MURDER BY MIDNIGHT

Jennifer Richardson

ISBN-10: 0692437215
ISBN-13: 978-0692437216

Library of Congress Control Number: 2015940311

Wild Romance Press, Waterford, New Jersey

DEDICATION

To my family and friends. Thank you for all of your support.

PROLOGUE

He was staring again. He had been glancing over at her all night, but had yet to make a move towards her. When she had first caught him looking at her earlier she had quickly, and shyly, looked away. But now that she had a few cosmos under her belt she was feeling a bit more daring. With liquid courage fueling her she caught his eye, smiled, and raised her glass in a silent salute before taking a sip. In response he mimicked her actions then slowly weaved his way through the crowd, his eyes never leaving hers.

Her heart sped up and she caught her breath. She had never been the type to pick up strangers in a bar, and now that he was walking towards her a wave of panic rippled through her body. *What do I do now?* she thought.

He stopped in front of her. His piercing, dark eyes searched hers as he took her hand and brushed his lips lightly across her knuckles. "Hello, my dear."

A thrill of excitement ran up her spine. "Hi," she said breathily.

"I apologize if I have made you uncomfortable, but I

just cannot seem to tear my eyes away from you." His voice was deep, soothing, and laced with an accent. One she didn't recognize. It washed over her like warm honey and her excitement grew. She had always had a thing for accents.

"No….it's fine. Really." Her voice trembled and she took a deep breath to steady her nerves.

"I cannot help but notice that you could use another drink." With his eyes still locked on hers he gestured for the bartender and ordered her another.

She didn't really want it. She was not afraid to admit that she was a light weight when it came to alcohol. She had already had three and her limit was usually two. Unfortunately, she just didn't know how to refuse, and the bartender had the glass on the bar before she had a chance to respond anyway.

Feeling that she had no choice, she picked up the pink concoction, raised it to her lips, and sipped. Its sugary sweetness flowed past her tongue and down her throat. "Mmmm."

He smiled. It didn't quite reach his eyes and a twinge of unease made itself known. Something just didn't feel right, and she scanned the crowd. She hadn't come alone. Her friend had to be around here somewhere. She had gone to the bathroom, but that had been a while ago. *She should have been back by now.*

Suddenly a wave of dizziness overcame her, and she brought her hand up and pressed it against her temple. What was going on? Placing the glass back on the bar she looked up to find him still smiling, but now his eyes were dark and cold. Unease turned to fear and she slid off the barstool, backing away from him. The ladies room was on the other side of the dance floor and she stumbled in that direction.

She almost didn't make it. The room was spinning and the strobe lights and loud music were wreaking havoc on her senses, but sheer determination had gotten her to the door. She was just about to push it open when a hand snaked around her waist from behind and a voice whispered in her ear, "you don't look so well, my dear."

She wanted to fight him off, but it had taken all her strength just to make it this far. She tried to scream instead, but when she parted her lips nothing came out.

Images of him clawing at her dress, the delicate fabric tearing beneath his hands, flashed through her head. She thought of those hands that were now at her waist touching her, caressing her, and her stomach roiled. "Please, don't do this," she managed to whisper.

"Why don't I take you someplace where you can lay down and rest?" With his arm still around her waist he pulled her up against him and guided her away from the door and the crowd.

Tears sprang to her eyes as she realized that no one would come to her aid. Why should they? There was nothing suspicious about a woman who appeared to be drunk being helped out of a bar. It happened all the time.

As the music began to fade, she found it harder and harder to keep her eyes open. *No!* She silently screamed. This couldn't be happening. She had always been so careful. She had thought she would be safe. How had he slipped something into her drink without her knowing?

"Here we are, my dear. Open your eyes." His voice, once exotic and exiting, now sounded sinister, and fear wrapped its cold talons around her.

She forced her eyes to open. She found herself laying on her back, something soft beneath her, and he was leaning over her. Reaching out he brushed her hair back, fanning it out around her.

Her tears were flowing freely now and he brushed them away with the pad of his thumb. "Don't worry. It will only hurt a moment," he whispered and the corner of his mouth ticked. A glint of something evil shone in his eyes.

Oh, god! She tried to raise her arms to push him away, but her limbs refused to cooperate. At that moment she knew she would never be able to fight him off so she steeled herself, waiting for his touch. When it came she sucked in a breath, her heart beating erratically in her breast.

He trailed his fingers along her cheek, tilting her head to the side and exposing her neck to his gaze. Then those same fingers traveled lower, coming to rest along the pulse point there, which was pounding out of control. A hunger like she had never seen before shone in his eyes and he bared his teeth.

Her eyes widened in shock and horror when his fangs appeared. And as he lowered his mouth to feed, her lips parted and she screamed with all she had.

CHAPTER 1

The oppressive, muggy air hung over the city as a thick white fog slowly rolled in to blanket the streets. The much needed rain had come and gone, but it had failed to cool things down. The unseasonably hot weather didn't stop the revelers, however, as they poured into the streets for another night of drinking and partying.

Celeste weaved her way through the throng of people, side stepping a group of drunk frat boys hooting and hollering at two scantily clad women on a balcony above. She rolled her eyes and ducked down a side street that was fairly deserted. *Spring break in New Orleans. It's a bitch.*

Most days she didn't mind the craziness. She enjoyed the jovial hum of the city as it passed her by, and the fond memories she had of walking its streets with her parents when she was a child. She had always loved the charm and magic that seemed to be New Orleans, and the wonder of it had always stayed with her. Even when her mother remarried after her father's death and her new stepfather had moved them to Boston, she had still dreamt of home.

Life had been good in Boston, but New Orleans never did seem to release its hold on her, and she had found her way back here after college. She had been lucky enough to be offered a job at a small local newspaper, and had settled back into the city as though she had never left.

In fact, that job was the reason she was here tonight. She was following a tip on a story that's deadline was coming up fast, and this was the first solid lead she had received. To say she was eager to get to her destination was an understatement.

As she made her way down the dark alley she clutched her purse tighter and glanced from side to side. The feeling that someone was watching her sent a chill running up her spine and she quickened her steps, breathing a sigh of relief when she emerged into another crowd of people. Surrounded by light once more she stopped and pulled a small scrap of paper out of her pocket. Pushing the mass of thick chestnut hair out of her face she studied the address then looked around.

She had traveled this street hundreds of times before, but had never noticed a club called The Lair. Where could it be? Shoving the paper back in her pocket she looked up and down the street then decided to go left, ignoring the lewd comments and leering stares of two men who stumbled past her. Trying to give them a wide berth she almost missed the small sign that hung over an unassuming door just across the street. Where most bars and clubs had bright neon signs declaring their presence, this was a simple nondescript one. It was almost as if they purposely wanted to go unnoticed.

Making her way across the street, pushing through the mass of people, she stopped in front of the door and took a deep breath. "Here goes," she mumbled to herself, and pushed open the door.

***

Alex watched the pretty brunette disappear into The Lair and shook his head. Peeling away from the shadows he followed her in. *She must be crazy. Or stupid.* Either way she was going to get herself into trouble.

The blaring music hit him as he swung the door open and stepped in, quickly melting into the crowd. Though a few curious eyes glanced his way, most ignored him. Good. He never liked to draw attention to himself.

Finding a spot near the back wall he scanned the crowd for the woman. She shouldn't be hard to find as everyone was dressed in black and wearing heavy makeup-mostly women, but some men too. With her designer jeans, high heeled boots, and red silk top she would stick out like a sore thumb in here.

As the band segued into another song those on the dance floor writhed against each other, seemingly heedless of those around them. Someone bumped against him and, turning to look, he found a couple urgently grabbing at each other. The man slammed the woman against the wall, pressing against her and driving his hips into hers. The woman, head thrown back, moaned as he sank his teeth into the creamy white flesh of her neck.

Turning his back to them, Alex focused his attention on the bar, expecting to find the woman there. She wasn't. Frowning he allowed his attention to be drawn back to the stage, and those gathered in front of it, hoping to catch a glimpse of her amongst the crowd. Then, from the corner of his eye, he spied a flash of red as it disappeared behind a black curtain hung along a wall by the stage.

Cutting across the dance floor he squeezed his way through the crowd, ignoring the multitude of hands that grabbed at him and tried to draw him into their orgy. Brushing them off easily, he reached the opposite side. Pushing back the curtain that the woman had disappeared behind moments earlier he found a long, narrow, dimly lit hallway lined on either side by closed doors. He stepped through.

As he made his way down the corridor he could hear the sounds of conversation and sex emanating from behind the doors. Unfazed by the activities around him, he purposely strode forward till he reached a dead end. He stopped. On his left was an exit door, but to the right the hall continued. Cautiously he peered around the corner.

Standing outside of an open door only a few feet in front of him was the woman. It was clear that she was trying to eavesdrop on the conversation inside. She hugged the wall, splaying her hands against it, and she was leaning to the side as though she was just about to poke her head around the corner. She had no idea of the danger she was in.

CHAPTER 2

"People are getting suspicious."

"Roman...Roman." He shook his head. "Relax my friend. You overreact." Leaning back in his chair he took a slow sip of his drink.

Pacing Roman said, "But there are some who have started asking questions ever since that girl went missing last week."

"Yes, but no one can connect her to The Lair. Really, Roman, relax. Have a drink. And will you stop that *damn* pacing?"

Roman didn't pour himself a drink, but he did stop and take a seat. However, relaxing appeared to be out of the question as he jiggled his leg nervously and began to tap a finger against the arm of the chair. "It won't be long before they connect her disappearance with that girl who went missing last month. And if they start looking further they will find out about the others." Roman shook his head. "What if they find out who is really behind all of this?"

Carefully placing his glass on the table by his side he leaned forward in his chair, piercing Roman with a cold stare. "They won't. And if you keep your mouth shut they never will."

***

They are talking about the missing girls. My contact was right! Celeste inched even closer to the doorway, trying to hear better. Maybe, if she could just get a little closer, she could get a quick peak and...

Before she knew what was happening Celeste was grabbed from behind, spun around, and pulled roughly against a rock hard chest. Before she had a chance to utter a single word the stranger lowered his head and began ravaging her mouth, pressing her up against the wall as he did so.

Celeste found herself momentarily paralyzed with shock, unable to fight off the stranger. As his lips continued to dance roughly across hers she finally came to her senses and, raising her hands up, she began pushing against his chest.

"What is going on here?" A gruff, familiar voice demanded as a dark figure cast its shadow in the doorway.

Looking up the stranger replied, "what does it look like?"

Ignoring the retort, the figure said, "Do it somewhere else," then slammed the door shut.

Celeste's heart was racing. *What the hell is going on?*

She wasn't exactly used to complete strangers grabbing and kissing her in dark hallways, and for the first time in her life she was speechless.

She had watched the interaction between the two men in stunned silence, then, when the door closed, the stranger released her, grabbed her hand, and quickly pulled her along behind him. Heading for a door marked *exit* at the end of the hall he pushed it open and hauled her out into the alley with him.

She was still in a state of shock. One minute she was standing outside the door, trying to get information for her story, and the next she was being mauled by some tall, dark stranger. Now he was dragging her along down a deserted alley.

Finally coming to her senses, and feeling panic begin to rise, Celeste dug in her heals and jerked her arm. "Let me go."

Stopping, the stranger spun around to face her, dropping her hand as he did so. Only inches away he loomed over her, his large frame blocking her escape to the busy street beyond. A chill ran up her spine yet again, but this time it wasn't accompanied by fear, though any sane person would be scared out of their wits at that moment.

"Who are you? And what do you think you're doing?" she demanded.

"At the moment I am trying to save your fool skin."

He had a hint of an accent, but for the life of her she couldn't place it. At the moment though it didn't seem to matter. "You had no right."

"The hell I didn't." He let out an exasperated breath

and ran a hand through his dark, wavy hair in an effort to find some patience. "You could have gotten yourself hurt or even worse in there. I most likely just saved your life."

Celeste rolled her eyes. "Oh, please. You're being dramatic."

He took a step towards her and Celeste instinctively took a step back. "*I'm* being dramatic?" He shook his head. "You have no idea what you stumbled into in there. What the hell were you doing there in the first place?"

Angered by this stranger's actions and words Celeste poked a finger in his chest. "That is none of your business." Turning around she reached for the door to reenter the club.

He grabbed her by the arm, staying her movements.

Infuriated now she spun around, eyes blazing. "How *dare* you? Take your hands off me or I'll scream. Don't think I won't."

Unintimidated by her words he growled, "Who are you? And what were you doing in there?"

"*Me?* I could ask you the same question." Uselessly she tried to pull her arm from his grip. "You are the one who accosted me without warning."

"I wasn't accosting you. If they had seen you lurking outside that door there is no telling what they would have done to you. There was no time to get you out of there, so I did the only logical thing."

"What? Mauling me?"

Giving her a shake he said in exasperation, "By making them think we were just another couple who couldn't keep our hands off each other. Believe me, they don't give it much thought as that's a pretty common scene in a place like that."

Still angry, and not willing to accept his so called act of heroism, she narrowed her gaze on him. "Why do you care?"

Releasing her he threw his hands up in the air. "At the moment I have no idea. If you insist on getting yourself killed, then by all means go right ahead." Angrily he turned and started down the alley. Celeste watched him walk away.

How dare this complete stranger decide what was and wasn't good for her? He didn't know her. He had no right. However…

Celeste's curiosity got the better of her, as it always did, and she called out, "Wait." The stranger stopped, but did not turn around. She debated for a moment whether or not she should tell him anything. She had no idea who this man was, but if she gave him a little information then maybe he would be inclined to give a little in return. With her mind made up she said, "my name is Celeste Boucher. I'm a reporter and I came here tonight because of a story. You see my contact told me that I could find-"

He was looming over her in an instant. She never even saw him move. *How did he do that?* Gripping her by the arms, he demanded, "Who is your contact? And what did they tell you?"

"Hey!" Celeste tried to wrench free. "You're hurting me."

He didn't let her go, but did loosen his grip. "Who is your contact?"

Fire sparked in the deep brown depths of her eyes as she met his cold stare. "Who the *hell* do you think you are? I don't even know you. Why should I tell you?"

"You want to know who I am? Fine. My name is Alexandru Razvan, my friends call me Alex." Forcing a smile he said, "Now that we are acquainted, Celeste, will you tell me who your contact is?"

"I can't." She shrugged her shoulders. "I always keep my sources confidential. If I didn't I wouldn't have any to speak of. That wouldn't bode well for the career you know."

"This isn't a game, Celeste. Tell me what you know."

"I don't know who you think you are, but I certainly don't answer to you." Finally wresting free, Celeste rubbed her arms and glared at him. "I'm out of here." Pushing past him she headed toward the busy street.

He was beside her before she even made it to the end of the alley. Surprised by his speed, she looked at him sideways with one raised eyebrow. He only shrugged.

"Look. It doesn't matter what you say, I am not going to give you the name of my source," she said.

In a smooth, charming voice he said, "then why don't we find a nice quiet place to sit, and you can tell me about this story your working on." Without giving her a chance to protest he placed a gentle hand on the base of her spine, and guided her towards a little café across the street that still had an open sign hanging on the door even at such a late hour.

"Wait a minute. How do I know you're not another reporter trying to scoop my story?" she asked.

Looking deep into her eyes he said, "I promise you I am not trying to poach your story."

The strangest sensation washed over her as she stared back into his eyes. She believed him. She didn't know why. He was a complete stranger and she knew nothing about him. But there was something in those dark blue eyes. Something that told her she could trust this man.

Nodding her head in acceptance she allowed him to open the door and nudge her inside.

CHAPTER 3

A short time later they were comfortably seated at a little table near the back of the café, a steaming cup of cappuccino in front of each of them.

Celeste nibbled on a piece of her Beignet and pointed at it. "Would you like a piece? It's delicious." As if to emphasize just how good it was, her tongue snaked out and licked her lips.

He watched the simple gesture as if mesmerized, a hint of a smile twitching at the corner of his mouth, then he tore his eyes away and looked down at his cup. Toying with the handle he shook his head. "No, thank you."

"Your loss," she said with a shrug.

"How about telling me about this story of yours, and what you know about The Lair?"

Celeste eyed the man sitting across from her. He was casually dressed in dark jeans and a black button down shirt. His inky black hair was slightly tousled, and he looked like he had just stepped off the cover of a magazine. Though he was comfortably seated-leaning back with one arm slung over the back of the chair-there was a tenseness about him, as if he would pounce at any moment. The man oozed sexuality.

The thought sent little shivers through her body and a slight blush stained her cheeks. This was ridiculous. She was acting like a giddy school girl out on her first date. What was wrong with her? This was business and nothing more.

Clearing her throat she said, "Well, it all started about a month ago when a girl named Julie Simmons went missing. I caught that story and wrote a small article about it. Her life, family, etc." She absently waved a hand in the air. "Anyway, last week another girl went missing, Beth Thomas, and I was given that story too.'

'At first I didn't give the two much thought. It was sad that these girls had just vanished, but I hadn't noticed any connection between them. Both grew up in different towns. Julie was from an upper middle class family and Beth was raised by a single mother just making ends meet." Her eyes lit up with excitement at her next words. "Then, two days ago, I got a call. I was told that there was more to both girls' stories then what met the eye. In fact, they actually did have something in common. They had both become involved in some underground vampire cult right before they went missing. I was told that I could find all the answers I needed at The Lair. That's why I was there tonight, to try and find the truth."

Picking up the last piece of the beignet she popped it into her mouth, closing her eyes to savor that last taste. Swallowing she opened her eyes, brushed the powdered sugar from her fingertips, and looked back up at him. "So, now that I told you my story, how about you tell me yours?"

She watched as he circled a finger around the rim of his cup. *Funny,* she thought, *he hasn't once taken a sip from that cup the whole time we've been sitting here.*

"My story is pretty simple. It appears as if we are both searching for the same thing," he said.

When he didn't continue she prompted, "Care to explain?"

"There really isn't much to explain. I was there tonight because of those missing girls too." Reaching into his pocket he withdrew a few bills and tossed them onto the table. Rising he walked over and placed a hand on her chair. "Why don't I walk you home? These streets aren't safe at night."

Rising she turned and stared up at him. "There has to be more to your story than that. What is *really* going on here?"

"I already told you. There isn't anything more to say."

She held his stare, trying to search the depths of his captivating eyes for anything that would tell her what he was really up to. Unfortunately, he gave nothing away. "Fine. I can't make you tell me, so I guess I'll just have to head back to The Lair and finish what I started earlier."

Celeste watched as his eyes grew darker.

"I have already warned you. That place is dangerous. Do *not* go back there."

"Give me one good reason why I shouldn't?"

Alex looked around, his eyes falling on the waitress behind the counter. Taking Celeste by the arm he walked her to the door. "This is not the place to discuss it. I'll walk you home and we can talk there. In private." Opening the door he ushered her out. "Where do you live?"

Celeste paused a moment. Could she really trust him? Was it wise to tell him where she lived? She had only known the man for the span of about an hour. That wasn't exactly enough time to really get to know a person. For all she knew he could be some crazy serial killer. In fact, he could have something to do with those girl's disappearances.

But then he looked into her eyes and she said, "I have an apartment on Esplanade. Just a block from Bourbon." The words fell from her lips before she even realized she had said them. Why would she tell him that? It was as if he had cast some type of spell over her and she was unable to stop herself.

He nodded and pulled her forward.

"Could we please slow down," she gasped out, trying to catch her breath as she practically ran to keep up with him. "It isn't far. There is no need to rush."

Alex slowed his pace and mumbled, "sorry."

Celeste caught him glancing around, keeping a wary eye on the revelers surrounding them. She knew that with so many people about it would be easy for someone to hide in the crowd and follow them without being noticed, though she couldn't imagine why anyone would. But judging by his actions, Alex seemed to think there might be a reason.

After his quick scan of the area she watched as he visibly relaxed, apparently not see anything out of the ordinary-at least for New Orleans that is.

CHAPTER 4

Rummaging through her purse Celeste found her keys and unlocked the door. Pushing it open she dropped both keys and purse on the small table by the door and breezed into the apartment. Walking to the center of the living room she spun around and pinned him with a no nonsense stare. Crossing her arms over her chest she tapped a foot. "Well, we're alone now. Are you going to talk?"

Alex stood just outside the door. "May I come in?"

Rolling her eyes she said, "Of course."

Slowly he crossed the threshold. Closing the door behind him, he took a few steps into the apartment and stopped. Placing his hands in his pockets he rocked back on his heels and looked around the small room.

Celeste watched him scan the apartment and looked around herself, trying to see it through his eyes. Granted it was small, but comfortable. The cream colored sofa dominated the room and was accompanied by a small coffee table she had picked up in an antiques store. A flat screen TV hung on the wall opposite the sofa and a desk took up the corner behind her. To her right was the small kitchenette which was divided from the living room by an island counter, and the door to her bedroom was to the right of the kitchenette.

Looking back at him she studied his face, but he gave nothing away. If anything he appeared to be indifferent to his surroundings. When his attentions turned back to her he said, "I don't know what more you want from me. I am nothing more than a concerned citizen."

"Bull. What are you really up to?"

"Alright. If you *must* know, I am an acquaintance of Julie Simmons's father. We had done business together a time or two in the past, and when I heard about his daughter's disappearance I wanted to help. I agreed to look into things." He briefly glanced down at his watch then back up at her. "I have a lot of connections in the city and I knew it would be easy for me to dig up some information."

She weighed this information, debating whether or not to believe him. His story was plausible, but why all the secrecy? Things just weren't adding up, and although she still had a million unanswered questions she decided to give him the benefit of the doubt. For now. "Fine. If that is true then what information have you dug up?"

He smiled charmingly. "I'll tell you mine if you tell me yours." She snorted in response and he let out a laugh.

Irritated with him now, she said, "I've already told you everything I know, now it's your turn." When he looked down at his watch once more, Celeste placed her hands on her hips and said in a clipped tone, "am I keeping you from something?"

"Actually, there is someplace I do need to be. I really am sorry, but I do have to leave." He gave her an apologetic look.

"Oh, no," she said shaking her head. "Before you go you have to tell me what *you* know."

Alex reached into his pocket and pulled out his wallet. Flipping it open he withdrew a small, white card and handed it to her. "Here is my card. Both my home and cell are on there. Give me a call tomorrow, and I promise we can talk then." He turned to leave.

"Hey, wait!"

"I really am sorry," he said over his shoulder, cutting her off. "Tomorrow." He opened the door and let himself out before she had a chance to respond.

She stared at the empty spot where he had been. *What just happened?* Groaning she threw herself onto the sofa and looked down at the card. His name was printed in bold, black script with his numbers in smaller print below. No occupation nor address were listed. Her brow furrowed. *How strange.*

After studying the card for a minute or two she realized that she wasn't going to learn anything from a phone number. She rose and went to her purse, slipped the card into it, and then began to pace. A lot had happened tonight and yet she had gotten nowhere. In fact, not only did she *not* learn any new information, but she ended up with more questions than when she started.

In frustration she flung herself back onto the sofa and turned the TV on for background noise. She hated being in a silent apartment. One of the late night talk shows was on and she decided to just leave it, there was nothing else on at this hour anyway. Curling her legs under her, she hugged a pillow and allowed her mind to wander back to earlier that night.

Whoever Roman and the mystery man were, they were the key to this whole thing. And what about Alex? Who was he? Was he connected in some way? She definitely had her work cut out for her now, and tomorrow she was going to do what she did best. She was going to do some digging.

**

Alex made his way back to The Lair in the hope that he still might learn something new, though he wasn't very optimistic. He wasn't too disappointed, however, as the night hadn't been a complete waste. He had met Celeste Boucher after all.

A wry smile twitched at the corner of his mouth as his thoughts strayed to her. She was nothing like he had expected. Though she was stubborn, reckless, and short tempered the woman was still captivating in her own way. She was strong and fearless, attributes which Alex admired and respected.

He had followed her coverage of the missing girls and had anticipated meeting her at some point to see just how much she knew. However, he had not expected it to happen tonight. In fact, he'd been quite surprised when he saw her walking, alone, into The Lair. He expected the woman to be tenacious-she was a reporter after all-but he hadn't expected her to be so foolish.

Back at The Lair, Alex once again pushed through the crowd to get to the bar. Getting the bartenders attention he ordered a beer, which he had no intention of actually drinking. He positioned himself at the end of the bar, so he could get an unobstructed view of the entire club. The band that had been on the stage earlier was still playing, and there appeared to be even more people on the dance floor-if that was at all possible- none of whom seemed overly suspicious.

Then, out of the corner of his eye, he caught movement at the curtain by the stage. A tall, well-dressed man appeared. The man looked familiar, but Alex couldn't recall were he had seen him before. He watched as the man crossed to the bar, leaned over to speak to the bartender, then crossed back and disappeared behind the same curtain he had emerged from.

Intrigued, Alex slowly inched his way toward the far wall. Shifting the curtain slightly he peeked around it and found the corridor empty, but before he could step behind it someone grabbed him by the arm and tugged. He looked down to find a curvy blond in a tight, black dress with flowing sleeves smiling up at him. Though she was attractive she wore way too much makeup, which made her resemble a clown. "Care to dance?"

Smiling politely Alex declined, but the woman's grip tightened on his arm, her blood red nails digging into his flesh even through the material of his shirt. Pouting she said, "oh, come on. Just one dance won't hurt."

Alex could tell, just by the look on her face, that she was the type to cause a scene if he didn't comply. Not wanting that to happen he allowed her to pull him out into the middle of the dance floor, where she began to move against him to the beat of the music. *Great!* he thought as he looked around, trying to find a way to extricate himself from the situation, but to no avail. Groaning softly he prayed for the song to end soon, which thankfully it did, and he quickly, yet gently, disengaged himself from her talons. He mumbled an apology and then foisted her onto the nearest guy.

Turning back to the curtained wall he found that it was now guarded by one of the large bouncers who policed the place. Realizing that he had missed his chance, Alex sighed. He knew he wasn't getting back there tonight. Reluctantly he headed for the door. There was always tomorrow night.

As he made his way through the crowd he was aware of a woman standing in the corner by the bar, her eyes intently following him. Though he was curious he didn't look in her direction for fear of spooking her.

He had seen her in here before, a few times, and wondered at her presence. The woman didn't belong here and if she wasn't careful she would end up just like the others.

Discarding his still full bottle of beer on an empty table, he left the loud music and the throng of inebriated people behind him. Once outside he slipped into the shadows and waited for the woman to exit. He didn't have to wait long. She emerged from the club moments after him and walked a few blocks before hailing a cab. Alex followed.

CHAPTER 5

The newsroom was pretty chaotic when Celeste walked in the next morning. She smiled to herself. The phones were ringing like crazy. There was that constant din of chatter, and people were coming and going. She really did love her job.

Going to her desk she picked up the phone and dialed her voice mail. Two of the messages were tips that she was certain wouldn't pan out, but she took down the information anyway. The other was a telemarketer. *These people are relentless.*

Deleting all of the messages she opened her laptop and got to work. Her first business of the day was to find out more about The Lair. Doing a search she came up with nothing. Odd. It wasn't too surprising that they didn't have a web page-even though most businesses nowadays did-but the fact that it didn't seem to exist anywhere was astonishing. She even tried the property assessment department and came up with nothing. Apparently, some big corporation owned the building, but there was no mention of a tenant. How could that be possible?

"Hey, sweetheart, what are you up to?"

Celeste looked up to find Joe Davis, her editor, walking toward her, a pleasant smile on his face. Joe was in his early sixties with salt and pepper hair and a kind, weathered face. Ever since Celeste had started working at the paper Joe had treated her more like a daughter than an employee.

"Hi, Joe," she said cheerfully. "I was just doing a little research."

Joe perched himself on the edge of her desk and looked down at the screen. "Anything new with that story of yours?"

"I've got a few leads that I've been looking into." She shrugged. "It's coming along."

"I hope it is. That deadline is coming up fast."

"I know." She rolled her eyes at his fatherly tone.

He put his hands up as if in surrender. "Alright. I won't mention it again." He placed a hand on her shoulder, his warm smile still in place. "You know Kathy has been asking about you. She's been wondering why you haven't been by for dinner lately."

Kathy was Joe's wife. Both Joe and Kathy had made her feel so welcome when she had first come back to New Orleans. She hadn't really known anyone then and they had welcomed her into their home for Sunday dinner, which had become almost a weekly routine. She had been so grateful to both of them for their kindness and Kathy's amazing cooking. Celeste herself could barely boil water, so that one night a week was heaven.

"Tell Kathy that I'm sorry. I've just been so busy, but I promise that I'll be there this weekend."

"Good," he said with a nod. "She'll be thrilled to hear it." He gently patted her shoulder, stood up, and walked to his office.

Celeste watched him walk away. She knew that Joe was right, Kathy would be thrilled. They had come to dote on her like she was one of their own. She didn't really mind though. Both of their children were grown up with families of their own, and they just didn't have the time to visit as much as Joe and Kathy would have liked. Celeste knew that she was the one who had filled that void for them, and she was happy that she could grant them that one simple pleasure, especially after all that they had done for her.

Sighing, she looked back down at her screen, her attentions focused once more on her work. After a few more searches she groaned. She wasn't getting anywhere on this damn computer. Sometimes a person just needed to do things the old fashioned way. A little bit of legwork always got the job done.

With her mind made up, she snapped the computer shut and reached for her laptop bag. Dragging it closer she accidentally knocked her purse on the floor, its contents spilling all over the place. "Great. Just my luck," she mumbled as she bent down to collect her things. As she scooped up her lipstick and some loose change she spied the little white business card peeking out from the corner of her purse. Shoving everything back in, she slipped the card out and studied it again. *Alex Razvan.* She tapped the side of the card with one finger as she thought, *who are you?*

She had always been a curious person, which was one

of the reasons why she chose journalism as a profession, and the vague card seemed to scream mystery. Not to mention that the man himself was an enigma. Deciding that her little trip to city hall could wait another few minutes she flipped her laptop back open and pulled up a new browser. Typing his name into the search engine she waited impatiently as the page loaded. *This thing is way too slow.* She was just about to pound the computer into little electronic bits when the page popped up and there he was.

Alex smiled back at her from the screen. He was dressed in a tux and was shaking hands with an older gentleman who was similarly dressed. They appeared to be at a benefit. Clicking on the link, she scanned the article that was associated with the picture, and found out that he had donated a large sum of money to a local charity for battered and abused women. *Impressive.* He suddenly rose one more rung on the ladder in her eyes.

Hitting the back button she clicked on the next link. This one mentioned a couple of investment ventures that he was involved in, but not much more. As she read a few more articles she found that he seemed to spread money around very generously, but none of them mentioned what he actually did for a living. Nor did they mention anything about family or even an inheritance. *So how did he become so wealthy?*

After searching for a half an hour she found she hadn't gotten anywhere new, so she gave up. Picking up the card once more she ran a finger over the raised print. Without giving herself time to think it over she impulsively reached for the phone and dialed his cell number figuring that would be the best way to reach him. He picked up on the second ring.

"Hello?"

"Um, Alex?" She asked hesitantly.

"Celeste? I'm glad you decided to call."

Now that she had him on the phone she didn't know what to say. How could she be so stupid? She should have thought this through first. "Uh, we never finished our conversation last night." As the words fumbled out of her mouth she winced, realizing how idiotic she sounded. Mentally she berated herself.

"You're right. How about I make it up to you? I know a great little Italian restaurant. What do you say to dinner tonight?"

Caught off guard by his proposal she responded numbly, "I…I guess so."

"Great. I'll pick you up at eight." He hung up.

Celeste stared at the phone. *What just happened?* She had called him with the intention of getting some answers and had ended up with a dinner date instead. How did he do that?

Joe, walking by her desk with a handful of papers in his hand, stopped and looked down at her. "Something wrong sweetheart?" He had removed his glasses and was studying her as if she had completely gone round the bend. At this point she was beginning to believe she had.

Hanging up the phone she gave him a crooked smile. "Nope. Everything is fine," she said, lying through her teeth. "In fact, I've got to get going. I have to head over to city hall to do a little research."

Seeming to accepting her answer Joe nodded and put his glasses back on. Fixing his attention back on the papers he said, "have fun," as an afterthought and walked away.

Celeste chuckled softly and shook her head as she slipped the laptop into its bag. Slinging her purse over her shoulder she checked her desk to make sure she hadn't forgotten anything then headed for the door.

***

Alex watched the woman as she exited the building and hurried down the steps. She briskly walked down the sidewalk, stopped once to look down and rummage through the black bag she held at her side, then continued on her way. After a few blocks she disappeared into yet another building.

He looked down at his watch and sighed. He knew that she would be in there awhile and he didn't have time to wait until she came back out. He had a meeting to get to.

He thought of canceling, but he had already put it off once and he knew that he couldn't do so again. Leaning forward he gave directions to his driver then settled back into his seat as the car started forward. He had some time before they reached his destination, so he went over the events of the night before.

Now that Celeste Boucher was involved he had to tread lightly. Things were definitely going to get even more complicated, and he was going to have to be more careful. She couldn't find out his secret.

"We're here sir." Roused from his thoughts, Alex looked out the window to find the car had come to a stop. Thanking the driver he opened the door and stepped out into the blinding sunlight. Though he was wearing sunglasses he still raised a hand to shield the light from his eyes as he quickly walked into the restaurant.

As his eyes quickly accustomed themselves to the dimly lit interior they scanned the room. He instantly spied the two men he was meeting and strode towards them. Seeing him advancing they both stood and held out their hands to shake his.

"We are so glad you could make it Alex."

"So am I." His tone was even. All business. Waving a hand towards the table he asked, "shall we get started?"

CHAPTER 6

As Celeste walked out of city hall she was more puzzled than when she had entered. After much digging she had found no record of The Lair. There was no business license. No liquor license. Nothing.

She was so frustrated she could scream. How could any of this be possible? The Lair didn't exist, and Alex Razvan didn't have a past. It was as if the world had turned upside down. What had she gotten herself into?

Shielding her eyes from the glare of the sun she looked back at the all glass façade of the multistory building that housed New Orleans's local government along with various other businesses. *So much for hands on,* she thought. Making a face at the structure, she turned and walked to the end of the block were she was able to hail a cab. Feeling defeated she sank into the back seat, gave the cabbie directions to her apartment, and fell into sulking silence. As she watched the city move by outside the window she mulled everything over in her head.

Her best bet of learning anything was tonight when

she had dinner with Alex. Unexpectedly, her heart skipped a beat at the thought of seeing him again, and she mentally chided herself for acting the fool. It wasn't like her to be so easily swayed by a handsome face. And what a handsome face it was. When he looked deep into her eyes it was as if he could make her believe and do anything. No man had ever affected her like that.

As the cab stopped in front of the little pink, two story house that housed her apartment, Celeste paid the man and got out. Climbing the two steps to the first floor gallery, she unlocked the door and trudged up the stairs to her second floor apartment. When she finally made it inside she dropped everything by the door, went straight to the sofa, and fell onto it. Closing her eyes she flung an arm over them.

She was so exhausted after a fruitless day of investigating that she just needed to rest her eyes a moment. She hadn't intended to nod off, but when she finally opened her eyes she found the room cast in shadows. Bolting up she looked at the clock on the wall. *Oh, no! It's seven.* She had dozed off for almost two hours. How could she have let that happen?

Rushing into the bathroom she turned the water on. Hopefully she would have enough time to shower, dress, and do her hair and makeup before Alex arrived.

Quickly undressing she reached into the shower to test the water then hopped in. She bathed and shaved her legs in record time. Hopping back out she toweled off and flew to her room to rummage through her closet. *What should I wear?* Pulling dress after dress out she tossed them aside, unable to settle on one. Why was it that no matter how many articles of clothing a woman owned she could never find anything to wear?

After she considered each dress-even the hideous, purple bridesmaid's gown she was forced to wear to her cousin's wedding-she settled on a simple black one with spaghetti straps. Slipping it on she hurried back to the bathroom to blow dry her hair and apply a touch of foundation, mascara, and lipstick.

When she stood back to look at herself in the mirror she was stunned. Though the dress had been hanging in her closet for some time she had never had the occasion to wear it, and hadn't realized how good it would look on her.

The silky material clung to her hips then flared slightly, falling to mid-thigh. The deep V neckline accentuated the swell of her breasts and the spaghetti straps showed off her creamy white shoulders. The only thing missing were her strappy black stilettos.

She couldn't help the smile that came to her lips at the sight. *Eat your heart out Alex Razvan.* As if on cue there was a knock at the door. Smoothing her hands down her sides she turned and all but sprinted for the door.

When she opened it she found Alex standing on the other side dressed in a tailored, black pinstripe suit. He cut quite a figure standing in her doorway and she stepped back to take him in. He did the same with her.

"You look stunning," he said, allowing his eyes to roam up and down the length of her.

The look on his face reminded her of the cat who ate the canary and she caught her breath. They stood that way a moment longer, taking in the sight of each other. Then, finally snapping out from under the spell he had seemed to put her under, she stepped to the side to allow him to enter. "Please, come in."

He did, brushing against her as he did so. Her pulse quickened and she willed it to slow. Why was she reacting like this?

"Are you ready to go?"

"Yes." That one word came out as almost a whisper.

"Are you sure?" His eyebrows rose and his gaze traveled down her body to the floor.

Celeste followed his gaze and found her hot pink toenails staring back at her. "Oh!" Her eyes flew back up to his and a slight stain colored her cheeks. "Let me get my shoes." She disappeared into the bedroom and emerged a minute later, stilettos encasing her feet.

"Much better," he said with a look of satisfaction. Offering her his arm he opened the door and walked her out.

As they exited the house a town car, complete with driver, was waiting at the curb. She raised a brow in mild curiosity, but remained silent. She shouldn't be surprised, really. From what she had gathered the man was richer than Midas. Why drive yourself when you can well afford to pay someone else to do it for you?

When the driver opened the door for her she smiled at him and slipped in, sliding over to allow room for Alex to join her. The car was roomy, but when Alex climbed in he seemed to fill the entire space. He purposely sat close enough so that his expensively clad thigh rested against her bare one, and Celeste, once again, felt her heart speed up at this contact. The urge to shift away from his touch out of self-preservation alone was great, but she fought the urge. She wasn't about to give him the satisfaction of knowing just exactly what he was doing to her. Instead she asked, "where are we going?"

"A little place called Antonio's. It's not far from here. I hope you enjoy Italian."

"Yes, I do." She thought a moment. "I tend to eat out a lot, but I don't recall a place called Antonio's."

"As I said, it's a small place and it's out of the way."

They fell into an awkward silence-at least awkward for her-as the car rolled along. She had a million questions for him, but didn't know where to start. Alex, however, appeared to be completely at ease as he glanced out the window and she fought the urge to groan out loud.

CHAPTER 7

Darkness had settled over the city and the streetlamps cast it in an eerie glow. Those who decided to venture out and sample what New Orleans had to offer mostly did so on foot, and for this reason there was little traffic. Before too long the car came to a stop in a quiet little neighborhood. The driver exited the car and opened the back door.

Alex exited first then reached back in to help her out. She was slightly taken aback by the gesture, and studied his hand a moment before placing hers in it.

Once on the sidewalk she looked up at the building before them. It was a small one story cottage that had been converted into a restaurant. A brick walkway, lined with flower beds, led to a porch adorned with hanging plants. A small plaque by the door read, in a flourishing scroll, *Antonio's*. Beneath that were the words 'fine Italian dinning'.

"Charming," she said, bemused. Alex smiled and held the door for her.

She stepped into a cozy little entryway. A pedestal

was just to her right, and a small man with black hair and a bushy mustache stepped out from behind it and greeted them. He quickly ushered them through a small dining room were a fire was burning brightly in the brick fireplace. Though only a few of the tables were occupied, he did not seat them at one of the empty ones. Instead, he led them through a set of glass double doors onto a small patio at the back of the building. The patio was just big enough for a handful of small tables, all of which were unoccupied, and he headed straight to the furthest one.

It was set for two. Candles at the center of the table cast a soft glow. Additional lamps were lit and placed about the patio. A row of hedges hemmed in the entire area, and a slew of ornate pots, filled with a riot of colors, were scattered about. It was a very romantic and very intimate atmosphere. Though a part of her was secretly pleased with Alex's choice there was another part of her that felt a little uneasy.

The maitre d' beamed at them. Clicking his heels he gestured to the table with an extravagant flourish. "Signore Razvan, your table." The little man then slid one of the chairs out for Celeste, who smiled warmly and thanked him as she took her seat.

"Thank you, Antonio." Alex took the seat across from her.

"Your waiter will be with you shortly." At Alex's nod, Antonio turned on his heels and hurried back into the dining room.

"That was Antonio?" She asked as she picked up the menu that had been placed in front of her.

"Yes. This is his pride and joy." Alex swept a hand out to include the building and patio.

"Hmm." She perused the menu, trying to decide what to order. Everything sounded so delicious she couldn't seem to choose. Glancing up at Alex, she asked, "as you're familiar with this restaurant, what do you suggest?"

Without looking at his own menu he replied, "the chicken fiorentino or the veal Genovese. Both are excellent."

Celeste weighed both options as she returned her menu to the table. The waiter that Antonio had mentioned quickly came forward and requested their orders. Before Celeste could respond Alex spoke up, "the lady will have the chicken fiorentino served over angel hair pasta with a glass of your best chardonnay, and I'll have the porterhouse, rare, with a glass of your house red."

As the waiter nodded and walked away she glared at him. "How did you know what I wanted?" she asked, irritation tingeing her voice. She had never liked the idea of a man ordering for her. She was a grown woman and could make her own decisions. Besides, it was very presumptuous.

He looked at her, amusement shining in his eyes. "I noticed the way your eyes sparked with interest when I mentioned the chicken. Not so much when I mentioned the veal. Therefore, I assumed you would enjoy the former rather than the latter."

"Well, I can speak for myself thank you."

"I'll remember that next time."

Next time? What made him think there would be a next time. Taking a calming breath she changed the subject. "You know, I was doing a little research today and found that you are quite a mysterious man." She said this with no shame. After all, she was a reporter. Her job was to research. He had to have known that she would.

"Ah, the internet age. It's virtually impossible to live the life of a recluse these days."

"*Actually*, it seems that one can. You practically *don't* exist."

He leaned back in his chair and raised a brow. "Really?"

"Yes, *really*. I found a few articles that spoke of your charitable donations and a few investments that you were involved in, but nothing about family or even your occupation." She studied him hard. "Who are you?"

"I thought I had already introduced myself," he said with a puzzled expression on his face. "Forgive me." He held his hand out to her and smiled. "I'm Alexandru Razvan. You can call me Alex."

She huffed and swatted his hand away. "I'm being serious." He was clearly amused and her frustration grew.

Sighing he said, "I was born in Romania. My parents died, leaving me an orphan, and when I came of age I found my way here to America. I worked hard at some menial jobs, saved my money, and then I took that hard earned money and made some shrewd investments. Now I live comfortably and I have the ability to help others when it's needed."

"That's it?" She looked skeptical.

"That's it. My life in a nutshell. Not as interesting and exciting as you expected is it?"

The waiter took that moment to return, their plates in

hand, and they fell into silence. When he left she unfolded her napkin and placed it across her lap. Alex did the same. Cutting off a small piece of the chicken she took a bite. He was right, it was excellent.

She looked up to find him smiling at her. "Good?" he asked.

"Yes," she murmured. Touching the napkin to the corner of her mouth she took a sip of her wine and casually asked, "what is your connection to The Lair?"

Alex sputtered, almost choking on the chilled wine he had been drinking. "My connection?" He shook his head. "I have no connection with that place."

"I find that hard to believe." She gave him a hard look then her face relaxed into a smile. "You know, I also learned something else today that is very interesting." She paused to take another bite. When she had swallowed she said, "it appears that The Lair doesn't exist."

She noticed that he had only taken a few bites of his steak and was now just moving the food around on his plate with his fork. When she spoke he stopped and looked up at her, his eyes cold and searching. "What do you mean?"

"I *mean*, there is no record of The Lair. I even went down to city hall, but found no licenses on file nor tax records."

"And what makes you think that I am involved?"

"Well, you were there last night."

"So were you and dozens of other people," he countered.

"Yes, but you have the means, and it's a fact that you are heavily invested in many different ventures."

"That may be true," he said, leaning closer. "But The Lair is not one of them." There was something in his voice that told her that this line of questioning was over. He was definitely not happy with what she was implying. She decided to heed his unspoken warning. For now.

"Alright, but the fact remains, on paper this place does not exist. The question is why?"

Alex relaxed back into his chair. "Well, that is simple enough. A lot of businesses don't operate above board, so to speak. It is not unusual."

"There is still something not quite right with that place." Finishing off the last of her wine she set the glass down and tossed her napkin onto the table. "I think that we should go back there."

"No!" His emphatic response had her eyes flying up to meet his with surprise. More calmly he said, "I already told you, that place is too dangerous."

Angrily she spat out, "Why? Why is this club so dangerous? What is it about this one that makes it so different from any other club in New Orleans?"

"Because, I know the type of people who frequent The Lair. They are....different."

"They're *different*! That's it? That's all you've got?"

"Celeste."

"No." Standing up she grabbed her purse. Anger rolled off her in waves as she said, "I am not going to sit here and let you dictate to me what I should and shouldn't do. What I should and shouldn't eat. For god's sake, I am a grown woman. And we hardly know each other for that matter. What gives you the right?" Spinning on her heel she stormed back into the restaurant.

***

"Celeste." Alex called out to her, but she continued walking away from him. "Damn it." Getting up he proceeded to go after her, but was stopped by Antonio.

"Signore, was there a problem with the meal." Concern was etched into the other man's face and he was wringing his hands nervously.

Alex gazed over Antonio's shoulder and saw Celeste storming out the door. Sighing he turned his attentions back to the small man. "No. The food was delicious," Alex said, reassuring him. Reaching into his back pocket he pulled out his wallet and counted out some bills. "Here. This should more then cover the bill." He handed the money over to Antonio.

Looking down at the generous amount Antonio shook his head. "This is too much, signore."

Alex clapped him on the arm and said, "it was well worth it," before walking past him for the door. Outside he looked around but found no sign of Celeste. The town car was still parked at the curb and Alex headed for it. "Did you happen to see the woman I was with leaving?"

He said to the driver as he climbed into the back seat.

Startled, the driver craned his head around to look at Alex. "Um…yes, sir, she went that way," he said, pointing out the windshield.

"Well, follow her then."

"Yes, sir." The driver quickly started the car and put it in drive.

A minute later they were pulling up alongside Celeste. Rolling the window down, Alex popped his head out and said, "will you please get in the car?"

"No," she said, without missing a step.

CHAPTER 8

Celeste refused to look at him. She was so mad she could spit nails. What was it about men that made them think that they always knew what was best? Well, she'd had enough.

"Celeste, there is no way you can walk all the way home in those shoes. Please, get in the car and we can talk."

Celeste stopped. Damn him for being so reasonable. He was right, she wouldn't make it home in these heels. They were pinching her toes like crazy. Her feet were already sore and she had barely made it a block, but she refused to give him the satisfaction of being proven right. Instead she looked at him and said coldly, "I will be just fine." Holding his gaze she slipped her shoes off then turned to continue down the sidewalk barefoot.

As she walked away she could hear Alex say, "I'll get out here." Then she heard a car door open then slam shut, and footsteps coming up behind her. *God, the man does not give up.* Without looking at him she said, "I am not getting in that car."

Alex fell into step beside her. He did not argue with her, but simply said, "I told the driver he could leave. You know, it's not wise to walk barefoot on a city sidewalk. There is no telling what you will step on."

"I'll take my chances."

"Suit yourself."

"Oh, lord! You just always have to be right don't you. Well, let me tell you…Ouch!" She stopped suddenly raising her foot in pain. Hopping to a nearby bench she plopped down on it, cradling her wounded foot in her hands. *Damn. Damn. Damn.* Why did these things always have to happen to her?

As she wallowed in self-pity Alex came up. Holding out his hand, palm up, he said. "I found the culprit." Celeste looked down at a sharp little rock resting harmlessly in the palm of his hand.

She glared at it as though it were pure evil, then plucked it from his hand and angrily threw it into the street. "Stupid rock," she mumbled.

Alex chuckled as he knelt down in front of her. Gently he took her foot in his hands and said, "let me see."

Celeste watched in awe as he tenderly rubbed the bottom of her foot, the pain and their argument from earlier were forgotten as his thumbs traced a circular pattern over the tender spot. Seemingly against her will, her entire body began to relax and she leaned back, closing her eyes in pure bliss. She knew that she should pull her foot out of his grasp, but his fingers felt too good. They were working magic not only on her foot, but other parts of her body as well.

Slowly his fingers moved up to her ankle then even higher to massage her calf. At that point Celeste gasped. Her eyes flew open and met his, which were dark with desire. His hands stopped and he lower her foot to the ground. "The rock didn't break the skin. You should be fine." Rising, he took her hand and helped her to her feet. Then, suddenly, he picked her up in his arms.

Shocked, Celeste blurted out, "what are you doing?" Instinctively she wrapped her arms around his neck, holding on.

"We don't need you stepping on another rock do we?"

"You…you can't carry me the entire way home."

"Are you implying that I'm not strong enough?" He raised a questioning brow.

Celeste groaned. *Oh, boy. Men and their egos.* "I didn't say that. I just meant that it's pretty far and I'm not exactly light."

"Are you kidding me? You're as light as a feather."

"Oh, please. Flattery will get you nowhere." He stopped and looked at her. As the silence stretched on she became more and more uncomfortable under his gaze and finally asked, "what?"

"Don't tell me that you think you're overweight." He began walking again. "What is with you women? It doesn't matter how skinny you are, you still think you weigh too much." He shook his head in disbelief. "Let me tell you something, Celeste Boucher, you are in no way overweight." Once again he stopped and looked at her.

"Got it?" She nodded. "Good," he said, and started forward.

Celeste looked at him as if she were seeing him for the first time. She had never expected such an impassioned speech from this man, and she didn't know how to respond to it. She smiled to herself and whispered, "thank you." Then said, for good measure, " this doesn't mean that I forgive you."

With her head resting on his shoulder she missed the amused grin that spread across his face.

CHAPTER 9

She thought that they would get strange looks from the people that they passed on the street, but oddly enough they hardly passed a soul. The ones they did pass didn't even give them a second look. *Just goes to show that nothing surprises people anymore*, she thought.

As he carried her up the steps, she was surprised to find that they had made it back to her apartment faster then she had expected, and he hadn't even broken a sweat or complained that she was getting too heavy. He had proven her wrong once again, and it was really starting to get on her nerves. Although, having a gentleman carry her to her door wasn't exactly a bad thing.

It wasn't until they reached her apartment door did he place her back on her feet, his hands lingering a moment as if he didn't want to let her go. When she met his eyes and caught a glimpse of the desire that she had seen there earlier, she quickly ducked her head, pretending to busy herself with finding her keys in her purse. The man certainly had a way of making her nervous.

Finding the keys, she fumbled to unlocked the door and then rushed in. Alex, not waiting for an invitation, followed behind her, closing the door as he went. The familiar clicking sound of the locking mechanism seemed to sound ten times louder than usual in the silent little apartment, and a cold chill washed over her.

It wasn't the fact that she was completely alone with him that caused her trepidation-she didn't fear him-it was the oddest sensation of...dread. She had a feeling that whatever he was about to say to her she wasn't going to like it.

She needed to break this uncomfortable silence and she wanted to put off whatever it was he was going to tell her, so she chose a subject that she knew would put her more at ease. Something that she felt would take her mind off of this feeling of dread. "You know, I'm still angry with you about what happened at the restaurant, and your little act of gallantry just now doesn't change that."

"I understand."

His voice was calm, even, and it drove her crazy. Why did he have to be so accommodating? She would love for him to lose his cool. Shout. Show any type of emotion. Unfortunately, he remained calm and collected, all the while making her feel like a petulant child.

Frustrated, she said, "and I am tired of all these secrets. I know that you know something and you are purposely keeping it from me. Well, I want the truth. I *deserve* the truth."

***

Alex stood there quietly listening to her tirade. When she finished-glaring at him with hostility-he slowly rounded the chair in front of him and took a seat. Looking up at her he said quietly, almost too quietly, "You won't believe me if I told you."

"Try me."

Alex debated whether or not to tell her. He wanted to, but self-preservation won out. Sighing he said, "you already know the truth, Celeste."

Rage seemed to rip a path straight through her, causing her whole body to tense and her eyes to shoot fire. She balled her hands into fists, then thrust her arm out and pointed towards the door. "Get out!"

Surprised, he looked at her puzzlingly. "I beg your pardon?"

"You heard me. I said, 'get out.'"

"Celeste-"

"No. I have heard enough. I am tired of your games. If you can't tell me the truth than you need to leave."

His eyes searched hers. Emotions whirled deep within them, anger of course, but something else. Something that quickly vanished before he could determine what it was. Could it have been hurt?

Sighing he rose and walked to the door. Turning back to her he said softly, "I really am sorry Celeste." Then, opening the door, he walked out.

***

Alex slammed the door behind him and stormed up the stairs, taking them two at a time. Once in his bedroom he tossed his jacket onto the bed and loosened his tie as he paced back and forth.

The truth. That was all she wanted. A simple enough request, and one that he wanted to grant her more than anything. But he couldn't.

She would never understand and he wouldn't expect her to. More importantly it was just too dangerous. It was safer for her to stay in the dark, even if that meant she hated him.

Flinging himself onto the bed he stared up at the ceiling. This evening had been going good. Great. Until Celeste had stormed out of the restaurant.

He couldn't help but smile at that. Even mad she was alluring, maybe even more so. And stubborn as hell. After all, what woman would walk barefoot down a city street just to prove him wrong? When she had stepped on that rock it had taken all he had not to laugh. But then, seeing her sitting on that bench, all humor was gone and he hadn't been able to resist the urge to touch her. The feel of her warm, smooth skin beneath his fingertips had been too much, and if she hadn't gasped at his touch, breaking the spell, there was no telling how far he would have gone. And on a public street no less.

Groaning, he sat up. What was wrong with him? He had never let a woman get to him like this before. Especially not enough to make him lose his head like that.

Feeling frustrated and needing some air, he rose. It was still early yet-at least for New Orleans standards-and the warm night was perfect for a long mind-clearing walk. Quickly changing into something more casual he hurried down the stairs, grabbed up his keys, and walked out the door.

CHAPTER 10

Celeste awoke to blinding light. She had forgotten to close the curtains the night before, and now the sun was shining through the balcony doors, directly into her eyes. Rolling over she buried her face in her pillow and groaned. Having to get up and go to work that day was the last thing she felt like doing, but she dragged herself from her bed anyway.

Glancing at the clock she decided that she would head out for a run and go into the office late. Maybe a good run would help to work off some of the anger and tension she was feeling. Changing into shorts and a t-shirt she tied on her old sneakers, pulled her hair back into a loose ponytail, grabbed her ipod and keys, and left the apartment.

It was such a beautiful day. The sun was shining, birds were chirping, and the smell of magnolias in full bloom wafted in the air. Looking around her, Celeste marveled at how the city had bounced back after Katrina. Granted, there was still a lot of work that still needed to be done after all this time and things would never be exactly the same again, but the city and its people persevered.

Starting to feel more relaxed, Celeste turned her face up towards the warm sun, a smile on her face. When she came to the end of the block she rounded the corner, heading towards Washington Square, and accidentally ran smack into someone coming from the other direction. Big, strong hands quickly reached out and grabbed her by the arms.

"Oh, god. I am so sor-" her eyes widened when she looked up into an all too familiar face.

"It's alright. No harm done," Alex said.

The tension that had begun to ease with her run now came back with full force. Anger shot from her eyes. "Excuse me," she said curtly, trying to disengage herself from his hold.

Alex didn't let go. Searching her face he finally said, "we need to talk."

"Do you plan on telling me what you refused to talk about last night?"

Sighing Alex looked away, his hands dropping to his sides. "I can't."

Throwing back her shoulders and raising her chin she said coolly, "then we have nothing to say to each other." Turning her back to him she jogged in the direction of her apartment, the run she had been enjoying now ruined by her encounter with Alex.

Why did she let him get to her like this? Why should she care so much? *Because it's your job to seek out the truth and find these girls justice. And, somehow, Alex is connected to all of it.*

Reaching the porch she opened the door and was just about to enter when a hand snaked around her upper arm and forced her to turn around.

She looked up into a face that was taut with anger. Fire flashed in Alex's eyes and he said in a low, menacing tone, "we need to talk, Celeste."

Apprehension snaked through her, leaving a cold chill in its wake. "I…I have to get to work," she stammered.

He gave a curt nod. "Tonight," he said. Without giving her a chance to respond he turned and hopped off the porch. He didn't look back as he made his way down the sidewalk.

Celeste stood perfectly still, watching as he walked away. She couldn't take her eyes off him. Even when he disappeared around the corner she continued to stare in that direction. It amazed her how one word, spoken with such authority, could make her feel both dread and anticipation all at once.

Shaking her head to break the spell she turned and stepped inside. Quickly running up the stairs she entered her apartment and went straight to the bathroom to hop into the shower.

Once she had showered and dressed she grabbed her laptop and purse. Heading out she opted to walk to the office instead of taking a cab. She hoped that the walk would clear her head so that she could focus on her work. But, unfortunately, by the time she made it there her thoughts were still a jumbled mess. She wondered how she would get any work done.

***

Alex sat on the bench beneath the shade of a large oak. A newspaper, opened to the business section, was in front of him. But he had no interest in the fate of the stock market, even though he was heavily invested in it. He had been around long enough to know that it was like a yo-yo, it may go down from time to time, but it always bounced back up. No, he wasn't worried.

What he was interested in though was the woman across the street. She sat with a bignet in front of her, sipping espresso and tapping away on her laptop.

As if sensing his eyes on her, she paused and looked up in his direction, but he wasn't worried about being recognized. With a ball cap pulled low, sunglasses in place, and the newspaper shielding most of his face, Alex knew that he would not be noticed.

After a moment she returned her attentions to her laptop, only lifting her head once more when the other woman walked up and slipped into the seat across from her.

Alex sat up straighter on the bench and concentrated on the new woman. *No! What is she doing here?*

CHAPTER 11

"Hello." Celeste scrutinized the young woman sitting across from her. She was fresh faced with long black hair, a slender body, and haunted green eyes. She looked wary, her eyes scanned the area around the café, and Celeste smiled to try and put her at ease.

"Hi," the young woman said.

Celeste had spent the entire morning working on her article, but had gotten nowhere. She had no more answers than she had the day before and her deadline was fast approaching. Frustrated she had been about to give up when her phone rang.

She had recognized the voice immediately. It had been the woman who had given her the tip about The Lair. When the woman had asked her to meet at this café her excitement had almost bubbled over. She had all but flew out of the newsroom and ran the two blocks to get here.

"You said that you needed to talk to me. That it was urgent." Celeste purposely spoke slowly and softly. Her tone gentle. Comforting.

Her tactic apparently worked as the woman began to relax. Finally the young woman spoke, her words a whisper, "I know the truth."

Celeste's heart began to beat a wild tempest in her chest. The answers that she had been seeking for so long were within her grasp. Taking a deep breath she said, "go on."

The young woman looked around then leaned closer to Celeste. Whispering she said, "I was there the night Julie went missing. I was at The Lair with her."

Celeste had not been prepared for this news. After speaking with Julie's family she had learned that Julie was a shy girl who didn't have many friends and didn't go out much. To learn that she had gone to The Lair was quite a surprise. "So you are a friend of Julie's?"

"I was."

Puzzled by the woman's choice of words Celeste asked, "what do you mean?"

"I *mean* that Julie is dead."

"Dead? Did you witness something? Why didn't you go to the police?"

The woman shook her head. "I didn't witness anything." Sighing, she leaned back in her chair. "Julie and I went to The Lair the night she went missing. I had been there a few times before-it was different and exciting-and I had finally convinced Julie to go with me. We were having a pretty good time listening to the music and watching the people dance, but then I had to use the ladies room." Celeste watched as the other woman's eyes glazed over as she remembered. "I told Julie that I would only be gone a minute, but on my way I ran into a guy I had seen in there before. We got to talking and I didn't realize how much time had passed. Finally, I told him I had to go and that I would talk to him later. I continued on to the bathroom and when I came out I noticed that Julie wasn't at the bar. I looked around and caught a glimpse of her before she disappeared behind a curtain with some guy. I tried to go after them, but some big bouncer stopped me. He wouldn't let me by no matter what I told him, so I waited and waited for Julie, but she never came back. Eventually it was closing time and they kicked everyone out. I had to leave, but I knew Julie had to still be in there."

"Why didn't you go to the police?"

"Humph." The woman shook her head. "And what would I tell them? 'Excuse me officers but my friend and I were at a bar and she left with some guy.' That happens every day. They would have probably just laughed in my face."

"But when she didn't show up and she was reported missing why didn't you say anything?" Celeste argued.

"Because I was afraid to. I had heard some crazy things about that place before I even took Julie there, but I didn't think much about them. To tell the truth, the stories made the place even more intriguing. But after Julie went missing I realized that those stories weren't just stories, they were true."

"But how do you know that Julie is dead. She could have just run off with him."

The woman stared at Celeste as if she had two heads, then said, "If you knew Julie, you would know that she wouldn't just run off with some guy. " She shook her head vehemently. "No. Whoever that guy was, he killed

Julie."

"Did you get a look at him?" Celeste asked.

"No. I only saw the back of him and it was fairly dark. He was tall, and well dressed. That's all I know."

Celeste sighed. That wasn't much of a description. "Alright. But why did you decide to come to me with this information?"

"Because I read your articles about Julie and that other girl. By the way you wrote I could tell that you cared." She shrugged her shoulders. "I figured if anyone could find out what really happened, and tell the truth, it would be you."

There was something about the way the woman spoke that puzzled Celeste and she asked, "what do you mean by that?"

"What I mean is…" Again, the woman leaned closer and lowered her voice. "Strange things happen at that place. Things that can't be explained. That's why I told you to go there, so you could see for yourself." Her eyes flicked up to watch a couple pass by the table. Once they had gone she whispered, "They are vampires."

"You mean, they are wannabe vampires."

"No. I mean that they are *real* vampires."

Celeste's mouth gaped open. She had not expected that one. Searching the woman's eyes she could see that the woman was actually convinced that there were vampires. *Oh Great. If she believes in vampires then what else did she make up? How much of her story can I actually believe?*

The woman leaned back, a blank mask settling over

her face. She must have sensed Celeste's reaction to her words. Not wanting to put the woman off, Celeste hurriedly said, "please, tell me more." But the woman clammed up, refusing to speak.

Celeste watched as the woman gathered up her things then rose from her chair. Celeste stood also. With one last ditch effort she asked, "can you at least tell me your name?"

The woman's eyes met hers then quickly flitted away. "I can't. It's too dangerous," she said, then turned and hurried down the sidewalk.

Sighing, Celeste picked up her purse and laptop bag. Turning, herself, she headed in the opposite direction than the woman. Back towards the office. She had work to do.

***

Alex watched as both women rose and walked off in opposite directions. Rising he looked from one to the other and groaned. He could only follow one.

Tossing the newspaper onto the bench he crossed the street and headed right. As he followed a short distance behind he watched as she stopped abruptly and turned down a lightly traveled side street. Quickly following he was able to catch up to her in no time.

Grabbing her by the arm he spun her around. Her eyes widened in shock and fear, and her mouth gaped open. Ignoring this he said, "I believe it's time we had a chat."

CHAPTER 12

By the time Celeste got home she was exhausted. Too many sleepless nights were taking their toll on her. Maybe she would stay in tonight, veg out in front of the television, and go to bed early.

Plopping down on the sofa she grabbed the remote and turned on the tv. The six o'clock news was already in progress, and the perky, blond weather girl was going on about the record high temperatures and how there seemed to be no end in sight.

Rolling her eyes Celeste tossed the remote onto the sofa next to her and grabbed up the take out menus littering the coffee table. Scanning through them she settled on a Chinese restaurant down the street that delivered, and picked up the phone.

Once she had ordered her Kung Pao chicken, she turned her attentions back to the news. The anchorman was now on discussing the upcoming Easter festivities and traditional parade, but she soon found her thoughts wandering.

She had really thought that she was getting somewhere when she met with the mystery woman today. But after the whole vampire thing she just didn't know if she could trust what the woman said. What part of her story was truth and what was fiction?

She played the conversation over and over again in her head until a knock at the door brought her back to the present. *Mmm dinner*, she thought as she jumped up and hurried to the door. As she opened it she turned to grab her wallet out of her purse. Taking out some cash she looked up and smiled at the delivery guy. "Here you go. You can keep the change," she said, taking the bag from his hands.

The fragrant aromas coming from the bag wafted up to tease her senses and her stomach growled in response, reminding her that she hadn't eaten lunch earlier. Quickly closing the door she placed the bag on the coffee table and removed the containers. "Great. They forgot my egg rolls," she grumbled as she searched through the bag. Sighing she went to the kitchen for a fork then back to the sofa, hungrily digging into the savory chicken. Heaven.

As she settled in for some mind-numbing vegging time with her trusty remote and amazing food there was a knock once again. Puzzled she looked up at the door then smiled as she rose. *They must have remembered the egg rolls.*

As she opened the door she said, "I thought you'd be back. Oh!"

Alex stood in the doorway dressed in jeans and a tight, black t-shirt that accentuated his well-defined arms and chest. His hair was slightly mussed, as if he had just run his fingers through it, and a crooked smile appeared. "I did say I would."

She had completely forgotten about Alex. How was that even possible? Lately, the man seemed to be on her mind day and night. In fact, he was the reason why she hadn't been sleeping. But her run in with the mystery woman today had monopolized her thoughts all afternoon, and had completely wiped her earlier encounter with Alex from her mind. But now it came back with full force.

"May I come in?" he asked.

Remembering the anger he had barely restrained earlier she wondered if it was wise to let him in, but after a moment's hesitation she stepped back, allowing him to pass. As he did so the phrase *curiosity killed the cat* popped into her head and she quickly pushed it away.

She watched him walk into the center of the room, and look down at the coffee table and her half eaten dinner. Turning to look at her he said, "I'm sorry. I didn't mean to interrupt."

She shrugged her shoulders. "It's alright. I was done with it anyway." The lie slid easily off her tongue and she wondered why she had said it. To be honest she hadn't even been close to done with it. She was still hungry, but thinking about the conversation that was to come, that hunger quickly vanished.

Feeling the need to busy herself she picked up the containers, closing them as she did so, and placed them in the fridge. The whole time she was aware of Alex's eyes on her, following her every move. As she closed the refrigerator door she took a deep breath and turned to face him. "Alright. You said you wanted to talk, so talk."

Nodding his head he sat down in the chair and gestured for her to take a seat on the sofa. She returned to the living room, but did not sit as he directed. Instead she took up a stance across the table from him. Folding her arms across her chest she stared at him and waited.

"I came here tonight because I need you to understand something. It's not that I don't want to tell you what you want to know. I really wish I could, but it's better for you if you don't know." He shook his head and leaned forward, bracing his arms on his thighs. "I am trying to protect you."

"Oh, give me a break. I am so tired of your cryptic words and your *need* to protect me. I am completely capable of taking care of myself. I have been doing it for some time now, and I don't need you barging into my life and making decisions for me."

"But you can't protect yourself against this."

"*This!*" She shouted throwing her hands in the air. "What is *this*?"

***

Alex knew that she had finally lost her patience with him. He couldn't blame her really. He would have felt the same way if he were in her shoes. The problem was, what did he do now?

If he didn't tell her then she would surely throw him out of her life and he couldn't allow that. She needed him whether she knew it or not. Especially if she insisted on continuing to look into those girls disappearances, which he knew she would. But if he told her…well, there was no telling what would happen.

His kind generally kept their identity a secret, and for good reason. If word got out chaos would probably reign. He knew almost nothing of this woman. Just her name and occupation, which was dangerous in itself. Could he really trust her? *Yes.* Something deep down told him that he could trust her. Trust her like he had never trusted another before. He made his decision.

"Alright, I'll tell you." He sighed and braced himself for her reaction. "That vampire cult, as you put it, isn't what you think it is. They aren't a cult. They are real vampires."

Alex watched her, judging her reaction. As he expected, she burst out laughing. Laughing so hard, in fact, that she doubled over, wrapping an arm around her waist. "That's a good one," she said, wiping at her eyes. "God, is everyone in this town delusional?" When she finally looked up at him she sobered quickly. He knew that his demeanor screamed serious and she had picked up on it. "Come on now. You seem like a normal, rational person, don't tell me you actually believe that."

"Yes, I do. In fact, I don't just believe. I actually am one," he said.

Unease wiped the smile from her face, and Alex watched as panic and fear set in. Wanting to put her at ease he rose and slowly walked towards her. "I promise you, I am not crazy and I won't hurt you." Raising his hands up in front of him, as if calming a frightened child, he said, "I really am a vampire and I can prove it to you. Please, let me show you."

Her eyes widened, and she took a step back. She looked like a deer caught in the headlights, ready to bolt at any moment.

He watched as the pulse in her neck beat faster and faster. The sound thrumming in his ears. Louder and louder. Ignoring it, he slowly reached out and took her hand. Raising it to his chest he placed her palm over his heart. Or the place where his heart should have been.

CHAPTER 13

Nothing. Celeste felt nothing beneath her palm. There was no heartbeat to be found.

Snatching her hand away she backed up until she felt the hard wall against her back. She expected him to lunge at her, but he didn't move. He just stood there watching her. Not wanting to believe, she fiercely shook her head. "No. No. It's not possible. Vampires do *not* exist." He had seemed like such a sane person. How could she have been so fooled?

Quickly glancing around she tried to locate her phone. Great. Why couldn't she ever just put the damn thing back where it belonged? Now she was stuck. She was alone in her own home with a crazy man who would probably attempt to drink her blood at any moment and she was unable to call for help. Maybe if she screamed loud enough the practically deaf, old woman who lived down stairs might hear her. One could only hope. *Way to go Celeste. You really got yourself in it now.*

"They do, Celeste. I do," he said.

"What are you going to do to me now?"

"I told you, I will not hurt you." Sitting down on the sofa he rested his elbows on his knees and laced his fingers together. He looked up at her. "Please, sit."

Feeling that it would be in her best interest to accommodate him-as the last thing she wanted to do at that moment was anger a crazy man-she slowly lowered herself onto the end of the sofa furthest from him.

She ran the events of the last few days through her head, replaying every moment she had spent with him. Some things that she had found odd were starting to make sense, however, some just weren't adding up. Could he be telling the truth? Was the mystery woman right? Tentatively she asked, "if you're a vampire, then why did you help me that night? Why didn't you just let them kill me?"

"Because, it's part of my mission."

Shaking her head in confusion she whispered, "I don't understand."

"I know that it's a lot to take in right now, and I'm sure you're having a hard time wrapping your head around all of this. Maybe you should get some rest. We can talk in the morning."

Her eyes flew up to meet his. "Are you kidding? You can't drop a bomb like that on me and expect me to just drift off to sleep like a baby."

"Celeste-"

She raised a hand to cut him off, then stared off across the room. She was sure he could see the wheels in her head spinning into overdrive as she processed everything. The silence dragged on, and just when he looked like he was about to open his mouth and speak, Celeste looked him hard in the eye, tilted her head to the side, and said, "I thought that vampires had to rest during the day? That you burn in the sunlight or something?"

Alex chuckled. "That is just a myth. You need to forget pretty much everything you have ever heard about vampires. Most of it isn't true." Celeste watched as the tension left his body. Relaxing some, he leaned back and placed an arm along the back of the sofa. "For instance, the sunlight doesn't kill us. We are extra sensitive to the light and prefer to limit our exposure, but we won't burst into flames or anything. The worst that could happen is a severely killer sunburn." He laughed, trying to lighten the mood. Celeste continued to stare at him.

"What about your fangs? Aren't you suppose to have fangs?"

Slowly, Alex leaned over until his face was just inches from hers. Opening his mouth he bared his teeth. Fangs instantly appeared.

Startled, Celeste squeaked and jumped to her feet.

Rising too, Alex held up a hand. "I'm sorry, I didn't mean to scare you."

"My god! It really is true." She began to pace, keeping one eye on him. She was definitely not going to turn her back on him now.

She tried to recall everything she had ever learned about vampires. Unfortunately, that knowledge was gleaned mostly from movies. Not a very reliable source. Still, images of blood-thirsty, soulless creatures flashed through her head and she suppressed a chill.

Stop it! Honestly, she really needed to stop letting her imagination run wild. She had to think rationally. In the short time she had known him he had been a complete gentleman. He had never once acted like one of those movie vampires, so why should she expect him to now? Besides, her instincts were never wrong, and ever since she had first met him they were telling her that she could trust him. Keeping that in mind, she decided to just come right out and ask him, "does this mean that you're going to drink my blood now?"

***

Though she was still clearly upset, Alex could sense that she was beginning to accept what he had told her. He had to give her credit, there weren't many women who would stand their ground after hearing that.

Surprised, and a little amused by her question, he said, "no. I'm not particularly hungry at the moment."

"That's not funny," she said, narrowing her eyes on him.

Sighing he said, "I guess that was in poor taste." He cringed. "Sorry, I was just trying to lighten the mood." Sitting back down he motioned for her to join him once again, and waited until she had done so to continue. "Actually, we try to get our blood through other means now. Mostly blood bank donations and willing participants. Even some animals if desperate enough. But

Jennifer Richardson

we do not drain people as we have in the past."

"Oh." She sounded a bit surprised and Alex smiled.

"My kind decided a long time ago that it would be advantageous for us to coexist amongst humans. In order to do that we had to take humans off the menu." When she cut him an angry glare he said, "*Wow*. You really are touchy."

"Excuse me, but the thought of being someone's dinner doesn't exactly put me in a chipper mood."

"Point taken. Anyway, once that path had been decided we knew that there would be those of us who would not be willing to comply. In order to enforce the rules a group called The Guardians was formed. Guardians watch over humans and hunt down renegade vampires. The Guardians are overseen by the Council, who pass judgment on us all."

"And you're a Guardian?"

"Yes."

He could see that she was trying to process all that he had told her. He knew it was a lot for one person to comprehend, and he hadn't even scratched the surface. Taking pity on her he said, "maybe you really should get some sleep. Things always look better in the morning."

"Oh, no. There is no way I'm going to bed now. I'm so jittery I'll never be able to sleep." To emphasize the fact, she rose once again and began to pace back and forth before him.

Alex sat back and watched her. He could see the wheels turning in her head once more. She was concentrating so hard he thought that the frown on her

78

brow would become permanent, and he smiled at the thought.

"I have so many questions, I don't know where to begin." Stopping she eyed him. "Is it true that a stake in the heart kills you?"

He narrowed his eyes on her, then that crooked smile appeared once more. "I don't think I should tell you. I don't want to give you any ideas."

Celeste blew out a breath and rolled her eyes.

Alex watched her reaction, realizing that eye rolling was second nature to her. She probably didn't even realize she was doing it half the time. "It is true. A stake will do the trick. And losing one's head doesn't help either." He shrugged his shoulders. "Other than that we are pretty indestructible. If we are injured we heal very quickly."

***

Celeste thought about this. At the moment, she was sorely tempted to drive a stake through his heart. *The man just told me that he's a vampire and all he does is sit there cracking jokes.*

She balled her fists in frustration. The panic and fear she had felt earlier was completely forgotten. She knew that she should run, get as far away from him as possible, but for some unexplained reason she felt safe with him. In fact, she was inexplicably drawn to him, and for the life of her she didn't know why. *I wonder if vampires can work magic too.*

"Okay. Let me get this straight here." She held up a finger. "First of all, you're a vampire." She held up another finger. "And secondly, that club we were at was a vampire club. Real vampires." She then held up a third and final finger. "And, lastly, you were there for the same reason as me, to find out about those missing girls." She threw both hands up in the air. "This is unbelievable."

As the words left her mouth she realized that it really wasn't. In fact, it all started to make perfect sense. Everything that the woman had told her was true.

"Yes, I can see how all of this would sound out there, but it is the truth," he said.

"Yeah, and sadly I believe it." Feeling deflated she sank down onto the sofa next to him.

"You are taking this pretty well," he said, purposely bumping his shoulder against hers.

"Gee, thanks." Looking at him she asked, "tell me about this mission of yours."

"There isn't much to tell. The Guardians learned of the suspicious disappearances of those two girls, along with a few others, and sent me to investigate." A darkness clouded his eyes. "There are rumors that a vampire called Dimitri has set up shop in our fair little city. He has been a thorn in our side for centuries, and many believe that he is behind all of this."

Celeste thought about this for a moment. She didn't recall ever hearing the name Dimitri, but for some reason she thought back to the conversation she had heard at The

Lair. "Dimitri," she mumbled, shaking her head. "I don't know anyone by that name, but…there is something about that conversation I overheard at The Lair. The nervous man didn't speak the other man's name, but the other man referred to the nervous one as…" She squeezed her eyes shut and thought a moment. "Roman!"

"Roman." Alex seemed to give the name some thought. "Dimitri did have a lackey named Roman. It has to be them."

"They are behind Julie's and Beth's disappearances! We have to call the police."

Looking around she tried to locate the phone once more. Finding it jammed between the cushions she grabbed it up and hit the talk button.

Alex reached out and clamped a hand over hers, preventing her from dialing. "No. We don't have any proof yet. And besides, if Dimitri is a part of this then we cannot go to the police. These are vampires, remember? We cannot involve the police."

"But-"

"It's just not possible Celeste. Vampires deal with their own. Humans are not to be involved for fear of learning our secrets."

She looked deep into his eyes. "But, you told me. You've involved me."

"Yes, but I had no choice. You've gotten in way over your head here, and I knew you would stubbornly continue down this path if I didn't stop you. Telling you the truth seemed like the only way to do that. If you don't give up on this story you will end up just like those girls."

"They deserve justice." There was such conviction in her voice, and Celeste saw a spark of admiration in his eyes.

"Your right. They do deserve justice and they will have it. You can count on that. Unfortunately, no one can know."

"But what about their families." The image of Julie's parents flashed in her mind. Mrs. Simmons crying uncontrollably, her husband trying uselessly to comfort her as he tried to hold back his own grief. And Mrs. Thomas, now completely alone and seemingly losing the will to live.

"I'm sorry, Celeste. It's just not possible to tell them," he said, shaking his head.

Celeste closed her eyes and rubbed at the ache that had begun in her temples. She had had a very long and eventful day, and it was beginning to weigh heavily on her shoulders.

Celeste opened her eyes and looked over at Alex. He stared at her with uncertainty. Then, hesitantly, he reached out and tucked a stray strand of chestnut hair behind her ear. Softly he said, "will you take my advice now and get some rest? You're going to need it." The uncertainty was now gone from his eyes, and was replaced by something else that shone in their dark blue depths. Something she couldn't quite figure out. But it stirred her deep inside.

Not wanting to acknowledge these unwanted feelings, she rose and took a few steps, trying to distance herself from him. Looking out the window she watched as a couple walked by on their way home from a night on the town. They were holding hands and laughing as they crossed the street and disappeared around the corner. They looked so happy and oblivious. If they only knew.....

The ache in her head steadily worsened and she closed her eyes for a moment. Sighing, she said, "Your right. I do need to lay down." Turning back to him she asked, "What about you?"

"I'll stay." When she raised a brow in question he smiled. "On the sofa. I don't want to leave you alone."

"I just learned that you're a vampire, and now you want to spend the night here? Even if it is only the sofa, you really expect me to be okay with that?"

"Celeste, I understand your misgivings, but I really don't think you should be alone tonight," he said, looking deeply into her eyes.

Warmth seemed to spread through her body at his words. She couldn't explain it, but for some reason she just couldn't seem to bring herself to tell him to leave. Once again she felt as if he had put her under some sort of a spell and the words just wouldn't come. Besides, she knew he would try to convince her to let him stay and she was just unable to find the strength to argue with him. So, she nodded her head in acceptance. "There are blankets in the closet." She pointed to a door across the room. "Goodnight." She turned and walked into the bedroom, closing the door behind her.

***

Alex smiled at the telltale click of the lock as Celeste shut herself up in her room. As if that flimsy lock could keep him out.

Sitting back on the sofa he replayed their entire conversation over in his head. When he had first told her that he was a vampire he had seen the immediate disbelief in her eyes, which he had expected. But then there was fear and that had taken him aback, even though it was warranted. He had never wanted to scare her and the thought that he had was disconcerting. Fortunately, he had been able to reassure her and she had relaxed, becoming quite inquisitive in fact, which had amused him greatly.

He had not expected her to be so accepting so quickly, even if he had given her irrefutable proof. She was stubborn after all, and seemed skeptical by nature. The fact that she trusted him, even after such an unbelievable story, touched him.

By the end, though, he had seen the exhaustion and what resembled defeat etched on her face, and it stirred something deep in his heart, which was ironic as he didn't really have one. The need to protect her had overwhelmed him, and he had been relieved when she finally gave in and decided to go to bed. It was funny, but he hadn't felt this way towards anyone in centuries.

Rising from the sofa he removed his clothes, and laid back down in only his boxers. Celeste had mentioned blankets in the closet, but he didn't bother. Temperatures didn't effect vampires too much, so he didn't feel the need for a blanket.

Laying there he gave some thought to what Celeste had told him about the conversation she had overheard at The Lair. Now he knew why the man he saw at the club looked so familiar. It was Roman. Alex remembered seeing pictures of him during his briefing with The Council, but had not made the connection while he was at the club. It was only after Celeste had mentioned his name that Alex realized who he was.

Now he needed to decide what his next move was going to be.

CHAPTER 14

Celeste closed her eyes and let the water slosh over her in a futile attempt to wash away the night before. If only it were possible.

It was hard to believe that only twenty four hours ago she was blissfully oblivious to the dark, sinister world that coexisted with hers. If someone had told her that vampires were actually real she would have laughed in their face. In fact, she had actually done just that. Now it was virtually impossible not to believe. There were just too many things that couldn't be explained to debunk the fact.

The question now was, what did she do with this knowledge?

The reporter in her was thrilled. This was the story of a lifetime. Every reporters dream. But deep down, she knew that she couldn't write this story. Alex had trusted her with his secret and it wouldn't be fair to him. Not to mention the repercussions that would follow.

She could only imagine how people would react. There would be panic in the streets. And there was no telling how the vampires would react to the fact that they were now the center of attention after centuries of living in the shadows. All of that probably wouldn't matter though because she would most likely be laughed out of town.

Turning off the water she threw back the shower curtain and reached for a towel, wrapping it around herself. Going to the sink she picked up her toothbrush and began brushing her teeth, her thoughts returning to the man sleeping on her sofa.

What was she going to do about him? The man-vampire-had got it into his head that she needed protecting. Well, she could protect herself. Even if she was going up against rouge vampires.

I can't believe this is actually happening.

Placing her toothbrush back in its holder she rinsed her mouth and looked up at the mirror, wiping the steam from its surface.

There he was, standing in the bathroom doorway. He was casually leaning against the door jam, arms crossed over his chest.

She knew she should have been startled at the very least by his appearance, or had been embarrassed by the fact that he was standing in her bathroom while she was practically naked, but surprisingly she wasn't. Actually, for reasons that were beyond her understanding, she expected him to be there.

What did give her pause though was the fact that she hadn't even heard him coming. He just appeared out of thin air. *How does he do that?*

"Good morning," he said, smile in place.

He acted as though it was just another normal day. She rolled her eyes. "Your still here."

"Yes. I told you that I would stay."

She continued to stare at him in the mirror and a frown began to form over her brow. "And I can *see* you."

"And I can see you too," he said, an amused smile spreading across his face.

"But I thought a vampire didn't have a reflection."

He pushed away from the door jam and waved a hand back and forth in front of the mirror. "Looks like you were proven wrong once again." He jammed his hands in his pockets. "Now that we've debunked that theory, did you sleep well?"

"No." Irritated, she pushed past him and walked back into her bedroom to rummage through her closet, the arrogant bastard following right behind. "Do you mind?" Snatching a pale blue summer dress off its hanger she waved it at him. "I'm trying to get dressed here."

Raising his hands in surrender he shook his head and left the room. When she emerged some time later she found him in her kitchen, lost within the depths of her refrigerator.

Poking his head up over the door he asked, "Breakfast?" He pulled a carton of eggs out and held it up. "I make a mean omelet."

"No, thanks. I don't have much of an appetite." Going straight to the coffeepot Celeste poured herself a cup of fresh brew.

"To bad. You have no idea what you're missing."

Alex returned the carton and closed the door, leaning back against it. He fixed his gaze on her.

Celeste took a sip of the steaming coffee, closing her eyes in contentment. There was nothing like that first sip of the day.

Opening her eyes she found Alex staring at her in amusement. Slightly embarrassed she quickly cleared her throat and tried to relax. Leaning a hip against the counter she wrapped her hands around the mug and asked, "speaking of food, you didn't eat much the other night, but you did eat. I thought vampires could only have blood?"

Unfazed by her question he responded, "we can eat food. But, unfortunately, it doesn't have much of an appeal to us so we generally don't bother, except for appearances sake."

"Then how do you know you make such a wonderful omelet?"

A sultry smile crossed his lips. "I've had many compliments."

Celeste rolled her eyes and Alex laughed. Placing her mug on the counter she crossed her arms. "So, what's the plan?"

Alex raised a brow. "The plan?"

"Yes, the plan. What do we do now?"

"*We* don't do anything," he said. "*You* get the hell out of town. Go on vacation or visit family for a few weeks. I don't care where you go, but get as far away from here as possible. And forget about your article. You can leave everything else to me."

"No. Oh, no." She shook her head vehemently. How dare he give her orders? He had no right. Straightening away from the counter she poked a finger in his chest. "I am a part of this now. You're not getting rid of me that easily."

"Celeste."

At his warning tone she said more firmly, "No."

Alex took one look at the stubborn set of her jaw and swore. Stabbing fingers through his already tousled hair he said, "Why can't you understand? This is an evil more powerful that you could possibly comprehend. It's too dangerous."

"Do you really want to know what I understand?" Tears, unbidden, sprang to her eyes and she fought to hold them back. "I understand what it's like to watch two mothers, their lives shattered because someone took their little girls away from them, clinging to that small sliver of hope that their daughters might come home. I understand what it's like to see the pain and anguish on their faces when they think of the horrible things that might have happened to their daughters, and the fact that they may never see them again. I won't just sit here and do nothing. I need to help them find closure."

Celeste could see that her words had moved him, and held her breath as he reached out to gently wipe the pad of his thumb over one single tear that had coursed down her cheek. Sighing, he softly said, "Alright. You win."

Turning her back to him Celeste quickly wiped at her tears, embarrassed that he had seen her at a moment of weakness. Trying to cover it up she busied herself with the task of pouring her unfinished coffee down the drain.

Alex patiently waited, giving her that moment to

compose herself. When she finally turned to face him again he said, "You can come along, but you have to promise to do exactly what I say and never leave my sight. Got it?"

Celeste was a little surprised by his words. She had figured that they would end up having a knockdown, drag out fight over it. She never imagined that he would cave so easily. Maybe those simpering women in the movies had it right. *Tears really do work.* Though she, herself, would never *intentionally* resort to that tactic.

With a somber look on her face, Celeste gave a single nod. "Got it."

Nodding himself, Alex walked across the room. Pulling a pair of sunglasses out of his pocket he put them on and opened the door. "Let's go," he said. Sweeping his arm in a gesture for her to proceed he ducked his head to avoid the glare of the morning sun and followed her out.

***

"So, what's next?" Celeste asked him as she all but skipped along the sidewalk beside him. Alex looked at her, the sunlight dancing upon her skin as it peaked through the branches of the old oak trees lining the street. Turning away he shook his head and sighed. He was really beginning to regret his decision to let her tag along.

When she had stood up to him with that fierce determination he had known that there would be no arguing with her, so he had given in. He had seen that look one to many times before from many a stubborn female, and he knew he would never win.

And then she had started to cry. Tears. How the hell was he supposed to argue with those? They were like the final nail in the coffin. When he had seen that single tear run down her cheek he felt the wall that he had built up around himself cracking. He just couldn't stand to see a woman cry. Somehow this woman seemed to always find his weaknesses and knew how to take advantage.

"First we head to my place. I need to change," he answered a little too briskly.

"Oh."

Alex could see the curiosity on Celeste's face. She probably thought that he slept in a coffin in some dark, dank crypt somewhere. The thought that he actually might own a home, and a nice one at that, probably never crossed her mind. Now he could see her mind racing with all the possibilities of where and how he lived.

At that moment he found himself caring a great deal about what she thought. He wanted her to see the home that he was so proud of. The one he had taken such great care to restore.

Suddenly he had the urge to get home as quickly as possible. Hailing a cab he opened the door and ushered Celeste in. Climbing in after her he said to the cabbie, "Seventh Street. The Garden District."

The cabbie nodded and the taxi rolled forward.

Celeste turned in her seat and looked at him. "The

Garden District?"

"Yes," he said.

At his curt response she shrugged her shoulders and settled back in her seat, and they continued the rest of the way in silence. When they turned onto seventh Alex said, "it's two blocks up on the right." The cabbie nodded once more and slowed his speed. When they came abreast of his white, second empire style mansion, Alex tapped the cabbie on the shoulder. "This is it."

When the taxi stopped Alex handed a few bills over to the driver, opened the door, and climbed out. Reaching back in, he offered Celeste a hand. When she emerged he kept his gaze on her face, judging her reaction. When she saw the house her eyes widened and she softly whispered, "Wow." Looking back at him she asked, a hint of disbelief in her voice, "This is yours?"

"Yes."

She let out a low whistle. "Nice."

"It serves its purpose." He said the words casually, but a surge of pride shot through him. He had put a lot of time and care into the house and her reaction made him realize that he had done his job well. Taking her arm he led her up the steps to the wide porch, and reached into his pocket to remove his keys. Opening the door he stepped back and waved her in ahead of him.

CHAPTER 15

Stepping through the threshold Celeste looked around in awe at her surroundings. "Wow!" she said once again. *And this is just the entryway!* "How long have you lived here?" she asked turning back to him.

Absently he said, "I've owned the house for over a hundred years now, but have only recently moved back within the last fifteen."

"A hundred years! My god." She narrowed her eyes on him. "Just how old are you?"

Alex thought a minute. "Oh, three hundred and fifty. Give or take a few that is." He waved a dismissive hand in the air. "I stopped keeping track ages ago."

Celeste's jaw dropped. "Three hundred and fifty? *Years?*"

"Yep."

She groaned. Was she ever going to get used to any of this?

Making his way towards the grand staircase in the center of the foyer Alex called back over his shoulder, "make yourself at home. I'll only be a few minutes." In the blink of an eye he was gone.

Celeste stared at the spot where he had just been mere seconds before. *Damn, but he can move fast.* Just another thing she had to get used to.

Deciding to forget that fact for the moment she settled on giving herself a tour. After all, she had never been in a vampire's house before.

It had never occurred to her that he would have his own place. In fact, when he had told her that he was a vampire she had wondered where he might live. She had certainly never expected it to be The Garden District. She had figured, instead, that he had some private crypt in the graveyard-there were plenty of those in New Orleans- and that he slept in a coffin. Thinking about it now she felt silly that she had even entertained those thoughts. *Although, he may sleep in a coffin.*

When she had stepped out of that cab and had gotten her first look at the massive house it had taken her breath away. It was a two story structure with a long porch that ran the length of the house and a small central balcony on the second floor. Large, arched windows graced both floors and a central pavilion jutted up at the roof.

She had had to drag her eyes away from it and look at Alex for confirmation that this house was really his. Not that he couldn't afford it-she knew that he could-but it was the fact that *he* lived here. It wasn't exactly a bachelor pad, and it definitely didn't scream vampire lair either.

Still deep in thought she wandered toward the back of the house and found herself in the kitchen. It was bright and welcoming. The perfect country kitchen atmosphere. It had glass front oak cabinets, granite countertops, and a small breakfast nook which looked out on the back garden.

Leaving the kitchen she headed back the way she had come until she was by the staircase once more. Eyeing the large doorway to her left she stepped through and found herself in the living room. Stopping she looked around and marveled at the elegance surrounding her.

Chippendale furniture was tastefully placed about the room, and a large Persian rug covered the pristine oak floor. Paintings-similar to the ones she had noticed in the foyer-hung on the walls, and studying one up closed she noted that it appeared to be an original Monet. *Who knew that vampires could have such great taste?*

Leaving the living room she made her way to the door on the opposite side of the foyer. This led to the library which, unlike the light tones of the living room and kitchen, had more of a darker color scheme.

Deep red mahogany floors were bare of rugs. Chairs, covered in dark brown leather, were positioned in front of a fireplace that dominated the wall to her right, and two large windows to her left let in just enough light so as not to make the room appear too gloomy. A large desk was positioned in front of the windows and contained only a laptop and phone, no papers or files littered its top. The two remaining walls were covered in floor to ceiling shelves, which were all but bursting with books.

It was a very masculine room and right away she knew that this was Alex's true domain. She could almost picture him sitting in one of the chairs, a book in hand, as a fire burned brightly in the hearth. Or sitting at the desk monitoring his investments. The mental images warmed her and she smiled to herself.

Walking around the perimeter of the room she trailed a finger along the spines of the books, noting the wide range of subjects from modern fiction to ancient Greek philosophy. Many of the tomes appeared to be very old, but lovingly cared for. There wasn't a hint of dust to be found.

She suddenly felt as though she was intruding and decided to leave. As the room had the feel of a typical library-it was quiet and seemed to demand respect-she felt the need to tread lightly. Tiptoeing back across the room she was careful to not allow her heels to click against the wood floor. Once she was there she turned to take one last look then softly closed the door as she left.

Finding herself back in the foyer she lingered, taking in the portraits on display. He still had not returned and she was starting to get a little antsy. She gazed up the stairs, but found everything still and silent. Biting her lip she looked away. Trying to distract herself she glanced at a pretty landscape gracing the wall next to her, but found that it couldn't hold her interest.

She glanced back up the stairs and that little devil on her shoulder urged her to go for it. *No!* She should stay put, wait for Alex. He couldn't be that much longer. But…

In the end her curiosity got the better of her and she slowly climbed the stairs.

At the top she found a hallway that branched off on either side of her. Opting to go right she slowly made her way down the quiet corridor, noting the closed doors on either side of her. Then she noticed the last door on the left was slightly ajar.

Knowing that she should turn around and go back downstairs she couldn't seem to make herself. Some unexplained force pulled her towards the door and she pushed it open, finding herself in the master bedroom.

Thick, black velvet curtains to her right blocked out the sun and cast the room in deep shadows. A huge bed, decorated in deep blues and blacks, dominated the center of the room and a large fireplace stood to her left.

Stepping into the center of the room she slowly turned in a circle, taking in her surroundings. As her attentions were drawn to the curtained doors that led to the balcony, she heard a creaking sound behind her and turned just as the door beside the fireplace opened and Alex emerged. Bare-chested with a towel wrapped around his waist, he walked right past her, without saying a word, and picked up a pair of pants laying on the bed.

"Like what you see?" he asked with his back to her.

Celeste could feel the color spreading across her cheeks at his words. She hadn't thought that she would come upon him half naked-at least not consciously. Maybe subconsciously though......*No! What is wrong with you? He's a vampire.* Angry now at both him and herself she lashed out the only way she knew how. "Oh, please. Don't flatter yourself," she said sarcastically.

He turned, smiled, caught her eye, and held it. Grabbing the end of the towel, he flicked his wrist and it fell to the floor.

Celeste gasped, spun around, and all but ran out the door and down the stairs. She could hear Alex's laughter following her as she went, and humiliation and anger roiled in her stomach. She was such a fool.

Once she was in the foyer she stopped to catch her

breath. Her heart was racing, and she chalked it up to her rapid flight from his bedroom. She refused to admit that it might have been his muscular body that oozed masculinity that had her pulse rising.

Once she had gotten her breathing and heart rate under control she began to pace. It usually had a calming effect on her and helped her think. She did it so often that sometimes she found herself pacing and not realizing she had even begun.

Today, however, it didn't seem to be helping. What was she thinking? What sane person would go hunting vampires *with* a vampire? And on top of that, what sane person would be turned on by a vampire?

She groaned. How could her world be turned upside down in less than twenty four hours?

"Ready to go?"

She looked up to find Alex descending the stairs. He was once again dressed in black. His hair, still damp from his shower, was tousled and his shirt hung unbuttoned, revealing a glimpse of his muscular chest and chiseled abs.

"Good god," she mumbled under her breath.

***

Alex heard her words, and he tried to suppress a grin. He thought about telling her of his heightened senses, which included hearing, but decided to save that one for later. She had suffered enough embarrassment for one day.

Buttoning his shirt as he walked over, he stopped just mere inches away from her. Looking down at her he was aware of her pulse increasing. The blood pumping faster and faster as it rushed through her veins.

A sudden hunger overwhelmed him, but it was not the desire to drink. It was a desire of another kind entirely. "Let's go," he said a bit too gruffly. Now was not the time. There would be plenty of time later to explore all the charms that Celeste had to offer, but right now they had work to do. They had to stop Dimitri-if it really was Dimitri-before another poor girl went missing.

Celeste didn't respond. Instead she walked past him, opened the door, and walked out.

Picking up his sunglasses and keys from the table where he had placed them earlier, Alex put the glasses on and walked out of the house.

CHAPTER 16

Celeste was standing on the porch looking out over the neighborhood. The Garden District certainly was a beautiful part of the city, and an expensive part too. She would have given anything to live here, but sadly she couldn't afford to.

That was okay though because she loved her home-a pretty Italianate style house that had been converted into cozy little apartments-and it was close to the office so she could walk to work.

She heard him close the door behind her, but didn't turn around to look. She was still trying to compose herself after the encounter they just had inside. She was certain her cheeks were still flaming, at least they felt like they were.

Taking a deep, calming breath she asked, looking straight ahead, "Now where?"

He walked up and stood alongside her. His eyes focused on the house across the street. "Back to Bourbon. The club will be closed, but I want to question some of the local proprietors, see what they have to say about their neighbors."

"Great." Turning her head she finally look up at him. "Are you going to call another cab?"

"Nope." He held up the keys and jingled them. "Don't need one." Hopping off the porch he rounded the house.

Following him Celeste found a sleek, black BMW parked in the small detached garage at the end of the driveway. "Do you own anything that isn't black?" she murmured.

He smiled and held the door open for her. She brushed past him to slide into the seat. The soft leather felt cool against her skin and she sank back into its comfortable embrace.

Still smiling, Alex shut the door and rounded the hood. Slipping in behind the wheel he put the key in the ignition and the engine purred to life. "Don't forget your seatbelt," he said, and waited for her to comply before he pulled out onto the quite street.

Celeste closed her eyes, leaning her head back against the headrest. *I could definitely get used to this.* The smooth ride and the soft purring engine was enough to lull a person to sleep, and since she had gotten little the night before she found it hard not to drift off.

***

Alex found a space outside the same little café where

they had talked the other night, and pulled up to the curb. Cutting the engine he glanced over at Celeste and found her sleeping.

She looked completely relaxed. Long lashes rested upon her cheeks and her mouth was set in a sultry pout. He couldn't recall ever seeing a more desirable woman and his hunger for her grew.

Needing to touch her he leaned over and traced a finger along her jaw and down the delicate column of her neck, lingering over her pulse point. The steady beat drummed against his fingertip.

At his soft caress she stirred slightly, a smile playing on her lips.

Bringing his lips close to her ear he whispered, "rise and shine."

At the sound of his deep voice her eyes fluttered then slowly opened.

Alex saw the surprise flash in her eyes when she found him leaning over her. With his breath warmly fanning her flesh and his hand resting just above her breast he had expected such a reaction. He also expected her to push his hand away and chastise him for taking advantage of her while she had been asleep, but she didn't. Instead, she remained still, desire now clouding her eyes.

He knew without a doubt that she wanted him to slide his hand lower. To lean closer, close enough to brush his lips against hers. Oh, yes. He knew exactly what she wanted, and he would have given anything to grant her that wish. Unfortunately, there were more pressing matters to attend to and neither one on them could afford the distraction right now.

Leaning back he removed his hand and rested it on the steering wheel. "I'm sorry to have to wake you, but we have arrived."

She looked around, as if just realizing that they were parked on a busy street, and a hint of color rose in her cheeks. "I should be the one apologizing. I didn't mean to fall asleep in your car. It's just that I didn't get much sleep last night and the seat is so comfortable and the ride-"

"There's no need to apologize," he said, cutting her off. "I understand." He knew his words had sounded a bit gruff and he took a deep breath, trying to tamp down the desire that had overcome him. When he felt in control again he exited the car. Celeste did the same.

They both walked into the café. The same girl from the other night was behind the counter, and when she heard the bell over the door jingle she looked up. Recognizing them she gave them a big smile and said, "You're back. What can I get you?"

"Coffee. Black," Celeste mumbled.

Alex smiled and said, "nothing for me, thanks." Pulling out his wallet he paid the girl for Celeste's coffee. Looking around the café he noted a couple of people spread out amongst the tables. The place wasn't busy at all at the moment.

Turning back to the girl he said, "You know, before the other night, I don't ever recall seeing this place here. Is it new?"

"Oh, we've been here for about a year now."

"Really!" He feigned surprise in an effort to keep the girl's attention. "Things must get pretty crazy around here with all those bars surrounding you."

"Sometimes, but that's okay. Business is business." She shrugged her shoulders. "We do get the drunks in here trying to sober up a little. Mostly their manageable."

Placing his arm around Celeste he smiled down at her then back at the girl. "The little lady and I have been down this way looking for a new place to party. We've gotten tired of the same old scene and wanted to try something new." He jabbed a thumb over his shoulder. "How about that place across the street? The Lair. Is that place any good?"

The pleasant smile vanished from the girls face and she wrinkled her nose. "That place is creepy." She gave a visible shake. "I know this is New Orleans-vampire Mecca and all-but the people who go in there are really weird, and they are always skulking about. If I were you I'd stay away from there."

"Then I guess we'll just keep looking." He gave her another one of his dazzling smiles. "Thanks."

"No problem. And don't forget to come back. We're always open." The young girl was all but drooling, and from the corner of his eye he saw Celeste roll hers. Looking at her he caught a glimpse of something in those dark brown depths. It was a flicker of emotion, but it was so fleeting that he wasn't sure he had even seen it. Could she actually be jealous?

Before he had the chance to give it any thought, Celeste abruptly turned from him and walked out. Looking back at the girl he gave her a wink and said, "will do," then followed Celeste out the door.

CHAPTER 17

The sun was hanging low in the sky by the time they returned to the car. They had spent the entire day going from business to business gleaning whatever information they could from those who worked there. They all had pretty much the same things to say about The Lair, both the customers and the employees kept to themselves and they were weird.

Alex had also found out that the club had only been in business a few months and the owner's name was Dimitri. No one could give him a last name, but it didn't matter. He knew in his gut that it had to be The Dimitri. The one he had been searching for. And he had no doubt that Dimitri was behind the disappearances of those girls.

Starting the car he turned to Celeste. She had been pretty quiet all day, which he knew was not like her. Even now she sat silently, refusing to look at him. Instead she looked straight ahead, staring out the windshield. "You look exhausted. Why don't I take you home so you can get some rest?"

"There's no time to rest. We should be going to the club," she said. Her tone was even, devoid of any emotion.

"The Lair won't be opening for hours. There's time." Putting the car in drive he pulled away from the curb and headed towards her apartment. They were there within minutes.

Finding an empty spot about a block up Alex slipped the car in, put it in park, and cut the engine. Exiting the car he came around and opened her door before Celeste could reach for the handle.

"Thanks," she murmured, barely glancing at him, and quickly stepping past him and up the steps to the door.

As they entered the apartment Celeste dropped her keys and purse in their customary spot, and kicked her shoes off as she walked over to the sofa. Plopping down she fell back and rubbed her hands over her face. "So, what happens now?"

"Now, you get some sleep."

She rolled her eyes. "I don't mean now. I mean tonight. What happens tonight?"

He smiled as he sat down next to her. "Tonight we go out for a night on the town."

She looked at him out of the corner of her eye, brow furrowed.

At her look he explained, "we go into The Lair as a couple." He was aware of her sharp intake of breath and suppressed a laugh. Continuing he said, "you see, the only humans who frequent that kind of place are vampire groupies."

"Vampire groupies?"

He looked at her as if he were patiently dealing with a child. "*Yes*. Vampire groupies. Humans who are fascinated and excited by vampires. Some of us vampires. Not me mind you, but some find this amusing and so they encourage these humans. Vampires like to bring their humans to these types of clubs, playing along with their fantasies." He looked at her arrogantly. "You are going to be my groupie."

Dropping her head back onto the sofa she groaned, "Oh, god."

Alex chuckled and slapped her on the knee. "Go lay down. We still have a few hours until we have to leave."

They both rose.

"What about you?" she asked, eyeing him warily.

He reached into his pocket and pulled out a cell phone. Holding it up, he wiggled it back and forth. "I have some calls to make." He smiled. "Don't worry, I'll be able to occupy myself. Maybe when I'm done I'll get lucky and catch my favorite soap opera on the television."

Shaking her head at his attempt at humor she walked into the bedroom, shutting the door behind her.

***

Collapsing onto the bed, Celeste stared up at the ceiling and watched the fan spin lazily around and around.

Though she was exhausted and knew she needed the rest, she just couldn't seem to close her eyes. Every time she did Alex's face seemed to loom over her, his hands running over her body and wreaking havoc on her senses.

The events of that morning replayed in her mind. Alex standing before her naked. Then later when she had opened her eyes to find him leaning over her, his hand resting over her breast. She had wanted more than anything for him to bridge that short distance between them and claim her lips in a searing kiss, but he had backed off.

At least one of us had some sense, she thought. How could she let her emotions get the better of her like that? She couldn't allow herself to fall for Alex. He was a vampire for goodness sake. What was she thinking?

Sighing, she rolled onto her side and clamped her eyes shut. Pushing all thoughts of Alex from her mind she tried to focus on the night ahead, and the role she would play.

A bit of unease began to creep up on her. For the first time today she began to worry about this plan. Was she getting in over her head?

All of Alex's warnings raced through her mind. She hated to admit it, but maybe he was right. Maybe she shouldn't have gotten involved.

No. She couldn't think like that. She got into the journalism business to find the truth. To tell peoples' stories. Those girls needed her.

Frustrated, she rose from the bed and went to the French doors. Ignoring the low murmur of Alex's voice as he spoke on the phone, she opened them and stepped out onto the balcony. Gripping the rail she closed her eyes and drew in a deep breath of fresh air, hoping that the sweet smell of honeysuckle and roses wafting up from below would help her relax as they usually did.

CHAPTER 18

Alex snapped the phone shut and swore. He had just gotten an earful from Sam Martin, head of the southern branch of The Guardians. Sam was the one who all the members down here had to answer to, and right now he was not happy with Alex.

He had told Sam about Celeste and how he had "outed" himself to her. Sam did not take the news well. The fact that Celeste was a reporter damn near drove him into a rage, and he had cursed Alex every which way for his foolish actions. He did calm down some when Alex told him of the progress he made, but the conversation still ended with Sam telling him to try to think more with his head and not with his dick.

Hearing movement in the bedroom he looked at his watch. *She should be getting some rest.* Going to the door he turned the knob and quietly opened it. His eyes went straight to the bed. Empty. Looking over at the open French doors he spotted her standing on the balcony, hair gently blowing in the breeze.

The sight of her standing there was too much to resist and he stepped into the room. He was behind her within half a second. Leaning close he whispered in her ear, "you should be in bed."

***

Startled, Celeste jumped and spun around. Thrown off balance she grabbed at his shirt, trying to find purchase. His arms quickly circled her waist, steadying her.

"I did not mean to scare you."

"I'm sure," she said sarcastically. He did not let her go and she was aware of her pulse quickening. Her skin tingled beneath his touch and her mind went blank. *Say something*, she commanded herself, then blurted out, "are you done with your call?" *God, I'm such a moron.*

"Yes. Unfortunately, my superiors are not too happy with me at the moment."

"Oh." Try as she might she couldn't think of anything else to say. *He must think I'm an idiot.*

Alex began to move his thumbs up and down her sides. "I told them about you and how you know our secret now."

The news should have worried her. The fact that vampires much more powerful then Alex knew who she was, and were aware that she knew their secrets, was not a comforting thought. Unfortunately, she couldn't seem to make herself focus on that. In fact, she couldn't seem to think about much of anything. Not with his hands driving her insane.

Slowly he slid those hands lower. "Though they do not forbid us from telling humans, they do frown upon it. And the fact that you're a reporter worries them a great deal. I reassured them as best I could." He began to scrunch up her dress, the hem rising higher and higher up her thighs. "I told them that our secret was safe with you."

She nodded her head, words failing her. Her heart began to pound in her chest and her knees felt like jelly. She fisted his shirt in her hands in an effort to hold herself up. When his fingertips brushed bare skin her legs all but gave out completely.

He bent his head down. His breath felt warm against her brow and she couldn't take her eyes off his lips. As she watched, those lips moved closer until they were hovering just over hers. "Don't worry," he said, his words a caress against her skin. "I won't bite." His lips finally brushed against hers. "Unless you want me to." Finally they claimed hers.

Parting her lips she took him in. Sliding her hands up his chest she wrapped them around his neck, thrusting her fingers into his hair and drawing him even closer. Then, pulling back slightly, she licked and nipped at his lower lip.

Alex tightened his grip on her hips and pulled her close. She was teasing him and she knew it was driving him crazy. He pinned her to the railing and reached up, snaking a hand behind her head and grabbing a fist full of hair. Gently tugging her head back he exposed the tantalizing flesh of her neck. Dipping his head down he ran his tongue along the erratic pulse that beat there.

At her sharp intake of breath he raised his head, his eyes searching hers. She knew that he expected to see fear and uncertainty in her eyes, but instead only hunger flamed within their depths. The sight seemed to aroused him even more because he let out a low growl and picked her up, carrying her to the bed.

All the doubts she had had earlier were completely washed away with each touch. Each taste. His lips and hands were driving her crazy and the need to have him inside her was all consuming.

When he laid her on the bed she drew him down with her, their lips never parting. Before she knew what had happened he had slipped her dress up and off, allowing the soft blue cotton to fall from his fingers and pool on the floor. Within seconds her bra and panties followed.

She lay completely naked under his gaze, and a thrill ran up her spine as his eyes roved over her body approvingly. All her life she had worried about her weight. She wasn't obese by any means, but she always felt she could stand to lose those few extra pounds. That's why, with previous boyfriends, she had always felt self-conscious. Not good enough. But not now. Not with this man. The way he looked at her made her feel like she was the only woman on earth. No one had ever made her feel that way before.

Reaching up she fumbled with the buttons of his shirt, groaning in frustration when her fingers would not cooperate. This elicited a chuckle from him.

He brushed her hands away and took care of it himself, tossing the shirt aside. His pants followed.

Celeste looked him up and down. *Impressive.* She had caught a quick glimpse of him that morning when he had purposely dropped his towel in front of her, but she had been so shocked and embarrassed that she had quickly fled before getting a good look at him. Now she drank him in.

There wasn't an ounce of fat on his lean, hard body, and well defined muscles rippled beneath his skin. Her heart skipped a beat then frantically pounded within her chest.

When he lowered himself over her once again Celeste wrapped herself around him, gasping as he thrust deep. As he moved within her, wave upon wave rushed over her and she held on tight, raking her nails down his back. When she finally climaxed she cried out, her body going taut.

She tightened around him as she found her release and he thrust one last time, following her over the edge then collapsing upon her. He lay there a moment, trying to catch his breath, then rolled over onto his back, drawing her with him.

Celeste lay her head on his shoulder, one hand resting limply upon his chest. "Wow," she panted.

"My sentiments exactly."

When her heart finally slowed and her breathing returned to normal, she raised herself up on one elbow and looked down at him. The hand resting on his chest began to move, and she idly ran her fingers through the light dusting of hair there. "I can't believe that just happened. I mean, I usually don't do this sort of thing. We hardly know each other-"

Alex reached up and placed a finger over her lips, silencing them. Then, reaching his hand around to the nape of her neck, he drew her head down for a kiss. Against her lips he said, "you don't have to explain. I know."

How does he do that? As frustrating as he could be, he always seemed to know just what to say. Just what to do. *Well, I guess he should, considering he's been around long enough.*

As his lips played against hers she slid her leg up along his. When her thigh brushed against his erection she pulled back and looked down at him questioningly. "Already?"

He smiled, "remember when I told you that we vampires heal quickly?" She nodded. "*Well…*" A sultry smile crossed his lips and amusement danced in his eyes. "Wounds aren't the only thing we recover from quickly." Rolling her over onto her back, he pinned her to the bed. "Let me give you a demonstration."

CHAPTER 19

Sometime later Alex lay in bed, Celeste curled against his side. After they had made love for the second time she had fallen asleep, exhausted. Unfortunately, for him sleep would not come. There were too many things rushing through his mind.

Celeste snuggled closer and he tightened his arm around her. Her hair had fallen in her face and he reached up to brush it back, tucking it behind her ear. She looked so peaceful.

He rubbed a hand over his face. What was he going to do? This stubborn, independent, frustrating woman had somehow wormed her way beneath the protective shield that he had erected so long ago, and he didn't know how he could ever walk away.

That was the problem. He had to walk away. He had learned the hard way that relationships between vampires and humans just didn't work. He had tried centuries ago and had failed, the pain eating away at him for years afterward. From that time on he had vowed to never let himself get too personally involved, and it had worked. For a few hundred years at least.

He had been able to keep his distance, never letting anyone get too close. On the occasion when he would get that itch he would find himself a vampire bar and some willing vamp who wanted nothing more than just a roll in the hay. That had worked for him, until now.

"Mmm" Celeste stirred. Opening her eyes she looked up at him and smiled. "I had the most wonderful dream." She rolled over onto her back and stretched. Alex propped himself up on his side and allowed his gaze to roam over her naked form. "I dreamt that we spent the entire day in bed. Not a care in the world. And you fed me an omelet."

He laughed. "I knew I'd get you to have one of my famous omelets one way or another."

Celeste sat up and reached for the robe at the foot of the bed. Slipping her arms into the sleeves, she tied the sash as she stood up and walked over to the open balcony doors. The sun had set and the night had cast its dark shadows over the city. "We have to get going." Closing the doors she locked them and turned back to him.

Alex glanced at the bedside clock. "We have time. It's still early yet. Things don't start getting interesting until later."

"Oh."

With her hair falling about her shoulders and her silk robe clinging to her generous curves she looked like an ethereal angel, and his worries of only moments before were swept away. "We have enough time to take a shower, if you want?" He raised a brow, a lazy smile playing on his lips.

Without saying a word Celeste walked across the room. At the door she looked back, catching his eye, and allowed her robe to fall to the floor before she disappeared through the doorway.

Alex was right behind her.

CHAPTER 20

They opted to walk to the club, leaving the car behind. Hand in hand they strolled down the street, appearing to all the world like any other happy, young couple. If people only knew.

Celeste had chosen a slinky dark blue dress and a pair of black four inch heels. As they made their way down Bourbon, Alex looked down at her feet and cringed. "Are you sure you'll be able to make it in those things?"

She dismissed his question with a wave of her hand. "Please. I'm a woman. We're used to suffering in the name of beauty."

"Then what happened the other night?"

She cut him a sidelong glare. "That was different. Those shoes were a bit too small and pinched. These ones fit just fine."

***

Alex shrugged at her words. Over three hundred years old and he still couldn't figure out why women insisted on torturing themselves in order to look good. Didn't they know that they could wear a brown paper bag and men wouldn't care? Though that dress was doing things to him......

He squirmed slightly, his pants feeling tighter. Trying to distract himself he said, "We should talk about a few things before we get there." He looked at her sideways. "First of all, you never leave my side. *Ever*. If they thought you were alone they would eat you alive." He stopped then and gave her a hard, stern look. "And I mean literally." She rolled her eyes, but didn't protest. He started walking again. "Secondly, you let me do the talking. If you start asking questions they'll get suspicious."

"Okay. I get it. You're in charge."

"Yes, I'm in charge. Remember that." They had reached The Lair and he stopped. Looking at her he asked, "ready?" She nodded her head. Opening the door he held it for her then followed her in.

The place was packed. The dance floor was crowded, as it always seemed to be, and the same band from the other night was on the stage. As they pushed their way to the bar, Alex scanned the room looking for Dimitri.

Alex thought of heading through the curtains to the back rooms in search of him, but he knew he couldn't leave Celeste. And taking her back there was out of the question. Instead, he gestured for the bartender and ordered her a glass of red wine.

Surprised she accepted the glass, took a sip, than shouted to be heard over the music. "How did you know I like red wine?"

"Didn't I tell you?" He leaned back against the bar, so he could get a better view of the room. "Vampires are psychic too."

Her eyes widened and her mouth dropped open. "Really?"

He laughed and shook his head. "No. I saw a bottle of red wine in your kitchen this morning and took a shot."

She smacked him on the arm. "That wasn't funny."

"The look on your face was." Movement of one of the curtains distracted him, and he watched as a man stepped out from behind it. Dimitri.

Alex's eyes narrowed on the man. As if sensing him, Dimitri turned and caught his stare, a slow smile crossing his lips. He gave Alex a slight nod, as if in greeting, but his eyes were black and cold. Without turning to Celeste, Alex said, "stay right here. Whatever you do, do not leave this spot."

She grabbed his arm, concern etched into her features. "Alex, what is going on?"

Flashing her a stern look he ordered, "stay put," and removed her hand. He looked back at Dimitri to find him gone, but caught a glimpse of a figure disappearing out the door. He rushed after it.

CHAPTER 21

When Alex had rushed out of the club, Celeste stood rooted to the spot as he had ordered. It went against everything she believed in to allow him to order her about, but after scanning the crowd she realized just how far out of her element she was. She knew that it was best to listen to him and not wander about.

She had been aware of the curious stares from those around her, and she had made sure to not make direct eye contact. However, she did catch sight of a young woman standing in the corner who was watching her intently.

As the lighting in The Lair wasn't the best Celeste had a hard time making out the woman. Squinting into the shadows she couldn't help but think that the woman looked familiar, then it hit her. The woman was no vampire. It was her contact. The woman from yesterday.

The young woman, realizing that Celeste caught her staring, quickly averted her eyes and turned toward the dance floor. Celeste went after her, catching her just before she slipped into the crowd, and grabbed the young woman's arm. The woman spun around, fear emanating from every pore of her body, and whispered urgently, "please let me go."

Celeste sucked in a breath. "It's alright. I believe you now. Please, let me help you."

The woman began to tug urgently against Celeste's grasp and looked frantically around the bar. "I'm sorry. You can't help me, and I can't help you anymore. It's too dangerous for both of us now. They know." Pulling free the woman turned to flee, but stopped. Slowly turning to look at Celeste she said, "I saw you with that man. Be careful. He isn't who you think he is." Turing once more the woman weaved through the crowd and disappeared out the door.

Celeste followed. As she opened the door she ran smack into Alex. He looked down at her, anger shining in his eyes. "I told you to stay put," he growled.

"I know, but my contact was here. When I caught her staring at me she ran out. I was just trying to catch her." Catching sight of the black haired woman she pointed across the street and said, "that's her."

Alex turned and, following the direction she indicated, he seemed to catch sight of the woman. Turning back to Celeste he barked, "go back inside. *Now.* I'll go get her." He opened the door and pushed her back inside.

The door slammed loudly shut behind her and Celeste stood there frozen for a moment. *Wait a minute. Why would he throw me back into the lion's den? Wouldn't I be safer outside?* Angry and confused, she spun around and flung the door open, stepping out into the night.

The street was well lit and she scanned it, her eyes

immediately going to the spot across the street where she had last seen the woman. She caught her breath. Alex had caught up to the woman and they appeared to be arguing. Alex had her by the upper arm, leaning over her menacingly, and the woman was shouting at him. After a moment, Alex tugged the woman closer and said something. At his words she fell silent then tugged her arm from his grasp. She backed up a few steps, her eyes never leaving Alex's face. She looked terrified. Then, turning, she hurried away.

Celeste quickly opened the door behind her and hurried back inside. Plastering herself to the wall, her mind raced. What had just happened? She had been too far away to hear what was being spoken, but both the woman and Alex had appeared as though they knew each other. How was that possible? And why did Alex let her go?

The door next to her opened and her head snapped to the side. She watched as Alex walked in, stopped, and looked around the room. As if sensing her eyes on him, he turned and smiled at her.

"Hey," he said walking over to her. His hand came out and circled her waist, pulling her close, then he dropped a kiss on her cheek.

"What happened?"

He sighed and said, "nothing. She disappeared before I could get to her. I'm sorry."

What!? Why is he lying? A sense of unease crept up on her. What did he know that he wasn't telling her?

Suddenly she felt the need to get out of there. Alex must have sensed it because he frowned, concern worrying his brow. "What's wrong?"

Smiling awkwardly she said, "I'm just feeling a bit creeped out in here. I want to go home."

Alex gently brushed a lock of hair from her forehead. He studied her a moment then said, "alright. Let's get you home." Turning to reach for the door he held it open so that she could pass.

Celeste quickly did so, not stopping to see if he was behind her as she started down the street. But Alex was immediately by her side, falling into step with her. He didn't try to take her hand or say anything. It was as if he sensed her change in mood and was respecting it.

They walked back to her apartment in silence. When they reached her door she stopped. Instead of unlocking it and going in she turned and looked up at Alex. "I…I'm really tired. It's been a long day and….and I just want to get some sleep." What she didn't say was that his actions had really thrown her for a loop, and at that moment she was afraid to be alone with him. After all he was a vampire, and the fact that he could be involved in all of this was becoming more and more of a possibility.

His eyes searched hers. He looked as though he was going to protest and she held her breath. She really wasn't up for an argument right now because she didn't think she had the strength to say no if he tried to push the issue.

Fortunately, she didn't have to find out. Though he looked disappointed he seemed to accept her excuse. "Alright, but whatever you do, do not allow anyone in. Okay?" Celeste nodded. Seeming to appear assured, Alex leaned forward and lightly brushing his lips across hers. He then said, "goodnight, Celeste."

His gesture was so touching, his words spoken so softly, that Celeste closed her eyes, unable to look at him.

She knew that if she looked up into those deep blue eyes she would be completely lost. She would never be able to send him away after that.

Taking a shaky breath she whispered, "goodnight," then turned and fumbled to get the key in the lock. Opening the door she quickly stepped inside and closed it behind her, not once looking back at Alex. Leaning against the door she listened for the sound of his footsteps on the stairs, but all she heard was silence.

CHAPTER 22

The next morning Celeste awoke frustrated. She had spent another restless night tossing and turning, her brain working on overdrive. It wasn't until dawn began to cast its deep purple and pink hues on the horizon that her body finally gave out and she slept, only to awake a short time later and unable to fall back asleep.

This investigation was consuming her like no other had done before. She couldn't sleep, she barely ate, and her stomach was constantly tied up in knots. And to top it all off she allowed herself to get involved with someone who may be a potential suspect. *What is wrong with me?*

Groaning she rolled over and looked at the clock. 7:30 am. She would usually be getting up at this time, but as it was Saturday she didn't have to go into the office. Instead she could relax. Sleep in. Unfortunately, it didn't appear as though she would be getting any more sleep.

Sighing she reached out and ran a hand over the pillow next to her. The same pillow that Alex had lain on the day before. At the reminder, images of the two of them played through her head like a movie. Alex touching her, tasting her, covering her body with his and driving her to heights she had never reached before with anyone. Then drifting off to sleep wrapped in his strong arms.

How was it possible to feel so safe and comforted by someone one minute, and wary and suspicious of them the next? What was this man doing to her? She had always been so sure of herself, but after meeting Alex it was as if she couldn't even trust her own instincts anymore. She just didn't know what to believe.

Realizing it was fruitless to lay there any longer she rose. Taking a quick shower she threw on a pair of jeans and a tank top. Not wanting to be bothered with doing her hair and makeup she grabbed her purse and headed out the door, her hair still damp and her face devoid of even a hint of lipstick.

She intended to walk around and enjoy the beautiful, warm, sunny day. She wanted to try and not think about work and Alex, just relax and have a stress free day. She would stop at her favorite café for a latte and beignet, then do a little window shopping. Maybe she would even break down and by those killer boots she had seen in the window of a little boutique she passed on her way to work every day. She had been drooling over those boots for weeks now, but she had resisted buying them because they were just too expensive. However, after the week she had just had she deserved a little pampering.

A short time later she was seated at a little table, a latte and beignet in front of her, watching the people as they passed by. She smiled. *So far so good*, she thought as she took a sip from her cup and picked up the paper she had grabbed from the newsstand across the street. *Same old, same old.* Everyone was pointing the finger at each other for the current economic troubles, and though they insisted that unemployment was declining there were still too many people without jobs.

Celeste sent up a little prayer that she still had work. Nowadays there were way too many newspapers going under, and she was thankful that her little local paper was still going strong. It just went to show that even though people couldn't live without the internet, they still liked the old standard. There was nothing like the feel of the paper in your hands and the smell of the ink in the air.

She sat there for a while drinking her latte and nibbling on her powdered pastry. When she was finished reading the paper, she people watched until the last crumb was gone and her cup was empty. She then went on her way.

When she reached the little boutique she stopped to look in the window. The boots were still there. Black, ankle high stilettos with a zipper up one side and a decorative buckle on the other. She quickly went inside and up to the counter.

A perky, fashionably dressed blond woman, who appeared to be in her early forties, stood behind the counter ringing up a purchase. Handing the customer their change she smiled and said, "have a good day," then looked at Celeste. "May I help you," she said, enthusiastically.

"Yes, actually. I would love to see those boots in the window." Celeste pointed to the boots.

The woman's face lit up as she rounded the counter and walked over to the window. Picking up the boots she asked, "these?"

"Yep," Celeste said.

"Excellent choice. These are so popular that I can barely keep them in stock, but I do believe I still have a few pairs in the back. What size?"

"Eight," Celeste said. The woman nodded and disappeared through a curtain behind the counter.

While she was gone Celeste browsed the racks, eyeing a white sundress then moving on when she saw the price tag. As she slowly made her way back to the front of the store she glanced up when she came to the window. She caught sight of two well-dressed men standing outside the restaurant across the street. They seemed to be having a serious discussion then abruptly stopped and greeted a third man who had walked up.

The third man's back was to her, but there was something familiar about him. He appeared to greet them with a curt nod and the two original men turned and proceeded him into the restaurant. But just before the third man walked through the door a car horn blew and he turned to look around.

Celeste gasped and her eyes widened in shock when she finally got a good look at his face. *Alex!* What was he doing there? And who were those two men he was meeting with?

"I found them." The saleswoman's words cut through the silence and, surprised, Celeste jumped and spun around. The woman, who was walking toward her with a shoebox in her hand, saw this and quickly said, "I'm so sorry. I didn't mean to startle you."

Celeste let out a shaky laugh. "It's okay. I've been a little jumpy lately." Shrugging it off, she took the box from the other woman's hand and opened it. The boots lay nestled inside, wrapped in tissue paper. Reaching in, she removed one boot, running her fingers over the soft leather. Sitting down on a nearby cushioned bench she slipped her shoe off and tried the boot on.

It fit like a glove and she smiled up at the woman appreciatively. Putting the other boot on, she stood up and took a few steps then inspected them in the mirror across from her. "These are great," she gushed, pivoting from side to side.

Sitting back down, she slipped them off, looked at the price, and winced. They were even more expensive then she had thought, but they had felt so good on her feet and they looked even better. Laying the boots back in the box she looked up at the saleswoman and said, "I'll take them."

The woman clapped her hands together and smiled. Taking the box from Celeste she said, "you won't be sorry. These boots are fantastic. Let me ring these up for you." She hurried over to the counter before Celeste could change her mind.

Celeste put her shoes back on and picked up her purse. As she walked over to the counter she whipped out her credit card and reluctantly handed it over. She sighed as the woman swiped it, and thought about the bill she would eventually receive. *Oh, well. These boots are well worth it.*

With the transaction complete, Celeste stepped back out into the bright sunlight and took a deep breath, soaking it all in. As she stood there though, she couldn't stop her eyes from wondering to the restaurant across the way. Though she couldn't see through the windows because of the glare, she knew that Alex was still inside with those men. What exactly were they up to?

Being curious by nature, the urge to walk across the

street, walk into the restaurant, and confront them, was too much and she took a step forward. But then she stopped. *What am I doing?* It was none of her concern. People met for business all of the time, and though it was strange that they would be meeting on a Saturday morning it wasn't exactly unheard of.

Celeste forced herself to continue down the street, but couldn't stop from looking back a few times before she rounded the corner at the end of the block. Though the restaurant was out of sight now it definitely wasn't out of mind, nor were the men inside it, and anger clouded her vision. *Damn that man!* She had been having a nice morning until she had seen him. She had even been able to push him out of her mind completely for a brief time. Wasn't it so typical of a man to ruin a perfectly good day?

She had been so caught up with her thoughts that she hadn't realized were she had been headed until she looked up and found herself outside of the newspaper office. It figured. Her job was so much a part of her life that she end up there even when she wasn't even consciously thinking about it.

Shrugging her shoulders she decided to go in. She knew that Joe would be there anyway, so it wouldn't hurt to pop in and say hello.

CHAPTER 23

Alex stepped out of the restaurant and looked down at his watch. It was still early yet. Things had moved along more smoothly then he had expected and his meeting ended earlier than he had figured.

Now he had other obstacles to tackle. The most important one being a mule-headed, little brunette.

He shook his head. He just didn't understand it. Things had seemed to be going so well yesterday. In fact, he thought that things were more than well. But then they had gone to The Lair. He didn't know what happened in there while he was gone, but whatever it was spooked Celeste. She had changed. It was as if she had suddenly become distrustful of him. What could have possibly happened in the few minutes he had left her alone last night that would cause this?

They needed to talk. He needed to know what had upset her and he needed to make it right. The thought that she might not trust him or even feel safe with him caused a sharp pain to rip through his chest like a knife plunging into his heart.

Pulling his phone out of his pocket he scrolled down till he found Celeste's number then hit send.

***

As Celeste reached for the door her cell phone went off. Rummaging through her purse she found it and looked at the screen. Alex. With her finger hovering over the screen she debated whether or not to answer, but before she could make her decision the phone fell silent.

Sighing she slipped the phone back in her purse, not even waiting to see if he left a voicemail message. She needed time to think before she talked to him.

Opening the door to the office she stepped into the newsroom, bypassed her own desk, and headed right for Joe's office. His door was open, as it always was, but she paused just outside of it anyway and lightly knocked on the door jam.

Joe was seated, intently studying a piece of paper. The desk in front of him was littered with a mountain of papers which were piled precariously high. In contrast to this, the rest of the room was meticulously neat. Books lined the shelves to his right, and an invitingly soft, leather couch was to his left.

At her knock he glanced up, a smile brightening his

face. "Celeste, what a happy surprise! I didn't expect to see you today." He placed the paper, which only moments before had consumed all of his attention, carelessly on the desk amongst the others. "Come on in," he said, gesturing for her to enter.

Celeste stepped through the doorway and into the office. Smiling she held up the bag in her hand and said, "I was just out doing a little shopping, was passing by, and thought I would stop in to say hi." Walking over to the couch she placed the bag down on it then settled herself next to it.

As she did so, Joe rose from his chair and walked around the desk. Pushing some papers to the side he cleared a small spot on the corner and perched himself there. Leaning forward he studied her closely, a frown deepening the wrinkles on his brow. "What's wrong sweetheart?"

"Nothing," she responded, her smile still in place.

He shook his head. "Come on now. You know I can always tell when something's bothering you, so spill," he commanded gently.

Celeste shifted uncomfortably under his gaze. Purposely avoiding eye contact, she focused on the family portrait sitting on the edge of Joe's desk. The happy smiling faces of Joe, his wife, and their two kids stared back at her. With her eyes still fixed on the happy family she heaved a sigh and said, "it's nothing really, I've just been a little preoccupied lately."

"Is it the story?"

"Yes…no…sort of." Not being able to sit still any longer, Celeste jumped up and started pacing. Joe continued to sit in patient silence, giving her time to collect her thoughts. "I sort of met this guy."

"Ah. I see." He chuckled softly.

Stopping in mid stride Celeste glared at him. The look was enough to cause most to cower and slink away, but it didn't even faze Joe. He had been the recipient of that look one to many times before for it to affect him. "It's not like that. Not really." Frustrated she stomped her foot. "What is wrong with men? Why do they have to make us so crazy?"

After a long pause Joe asked, "was that a rhetorical question or am I supposed to answer that?"

Groaning, Celeste plopped back down on the couch, which caused the shopping bag to tip over. "I'm just so confused." Meeting Joe's gentle gaze she explained, "you see, I met this guy, Alex, while working on this story. He's been helping me, but now I think that he knows more than he's telling me. I just don't know what to believe anymore."

"Well, do you trust him?" When she didn't answer his question, Joe rose from his perch to kneel in front of her. Taking up one of her hands he gave it a gentle squeeze and asked softly, "what does your gut say?"

Closing her eyes she whispered, "yes."

"Well then, I guess it's settled."

Opening her eyes, Celeste watched as Joe rose and returned to his desk chair. Settling into it, he picked up the paper he had discarded when she had first entered the office and glanced down at it. Without looking back up at her he said, "don't forget, Kathy's expecting you for dinner tomorrow."

Smiling Celeste shook her head. Leave it to Joe to make the most confusing situation seem so simple. Rising herself, she picked up her purse and shopping bag, and headed for the door. "Thanks Joe," she threw over her shoulder.

Just before she walked out the door, Joe's voice stopped her. "Why don't you bring your gentleman friend with you?"

Spinning around she stared at him openmouthed, but Joe was intently studying that piece of paper. "Joe, I don't think I should. Kathy-"

Without looking up, Joe waved a hand in the air to silence her. "Kathy will be ecstatic. The more the merrier she always says."

Celeste continued to stare at him trying to rack her brain for a good excuse, but how could she possibly tell him that she couldn't bring Alex without explaining that he was a vampire. *Sorry Joe, but he doesn't really eat food. He only drinks blood.* Yeah, that would go over well. They would probably have her committed.

Stumped, she found herself saying, "alright. I'll ask him to come." At Joe's nod, Celeste spun around and hurried out the door.

CHAPTER 24

Celeste spent the next hour walking around and thinking. Maybe Joe was right. Maybe all she needed to do was listen to her gut. It had always come through for her before, so why should this time be any different?

What she needed to do was talk to Alex. Stepping out of the way of the foot traffic surrounding her, Celeste reached into her purse and dug out her phone. She looked down at a blank screen. "Damn," she swore a little too loudly, eliciting a startled look from the elderly woman who had just exited the shop a few feet away. Ignoring the woman, Celeste began to angrily hit the power button, but to no avail. The battery was dead.

Frustrated she rammed the phone back into her purse. She would just have to wait till she got home and call him from there. Not wanting to waste any time she headed in that direction, her steps quickening the closer she got.

A few minutes later, as she rounded the corner at the end of her block, she could just make out two figures sitting in the wicker rockers on her front porch. As she got closer she was surprised to find Mrs. Stanford, the elderly woman who lived downstairs, chatting away with none other than Alex.

As she came up the walk, Alex spied her and smiled. He rose as she made her way up the steps onto the porch.

"Why, hello dear," Mrs. Stanford greeted, beaming up at Celeste.

"Hello Mrs. Stanford," Celeste greeted loudly. Mrs. Stanford was a sweet, cheery woman in her mid-eighties who, unfortunately, had trouble hearing, but refused to wear her hearing aides.

"Your young man here has been keeping me company."

"And I have enjoyed every minute of it," Alex said, flashing Mrs. Stanford one of his dazzling smiles, which caused the older woman to blush. Looking back at Celeste he said, "Mrs. Stanford was kind enough to share some of her delicious sweet tea." He held up the glass and took a sip then placed it on the table between the rockers, thanking Mrs. Stanford as he did so.

"It was my pleasure," she replied. "After all it's not every day that a handsome young man takes the time to sit and chat with an old woman like myself."

"Old? Why, you don't look a day over thirty."

Celeste couldn't help but smile as the older woman's cheeks reddened once again at Alex's compliment.

"Oh, you," Mrs. Stanford said, waving a hand in his direction. Looking at Celeste she said, "why don't you two run along now." She gave Celeste a knowing smile.

This time it was Celeste's turn to blush. Embarrassed, she turned and distracted herself with the task of opening the door. After a bit of fumbling with the handle the door swung open. Turning back to the old woman she said, "if there is anything you need let me know."

"Oh, don't worry 'bout me dear. I'm fine." Leaning back, Mrs. Stanford closed her eyes and began rocking, a smile softening her weathered features.

Celeste stepped inside and headed up the stairs knowing that Alex was directly behind her. At her apartment she unlocked the door and pushed her way in, immediately dropping her keys and purse by the door.

Without looking at Alex she continued on to the bedroom, saying over her shoulder, "let me just put this bag away."

She didn't need to, really, she just wanted an extra minute or two to gather her thoughts before confronting him. Placing the bag in her closet she turned back to the door, took a deep breath, and walked back out into the living room.

Alex was there, sitting in the armchair patiently waiting, his face a blank mask. As hard as she tried she couldn't figure out what he was thinking.

Taking a seat on the sofa she looked at him and casually asked, "so, what did you do this morning?" Tensely she awaited his reply.

A flicker of surprise flashed in his eyes at her question, but instantly vanished. "I was at home. Working."

"So you didn't get out and enjoy this beautiful day?"

Celeste watched Alex closely. He continued to sit there calmly. The only outward sign of his discomfort was the fact that he was fidgeting with the cuff of his sleeve.

"Unfortunately, I did not. I was very busy this morning." His voice sounded smooth and even, and she had to admit that he was good. Unfortunately, for her that was a bad thing. She knew for a fact that he hadn't been home. That she had seen him at the restaurant with those two men. Why was he lying? What was he trying to hide from her?

As these questions raced through her brain, her suspicions grew. Last night he had lied to her about the young woman. He had caught up to her, and it was clear by the way they were arguing that they had met before. And now he was lying about his whereabouts this morning.

She had told Joe that she believed she could trust Alex, but her doubts continued to mount. So, why was it that deep down she still believed she could?

When she looked back at Alex she found him studying her. His eyes narrowed on her and it felt as though he could read her thoughts. Uncomfortable under his scrutiny she quickly got to her feet and walked over to the window. Nervously she lifted a hand to brush back the curtain and look down onto the busy street outside.

The silence seemed to stretch on between them. Then, finally, Alex's rich, deep voice broke the quiet. "What is bothering you Celeste?"

Without turning to look at him she softly said, "I saw you this morning."

She expected him to respond, but silence filled the small room. After a moment she turned to face him. He was still sitting in the armchair, but a smile had settled on his lips. His eyes seemed to dance with amusement as they rested on her.

Frustrated by his reaction to her admission she demanded, "aren't you going to say anything?"

Slowly and fluidly Alex rose from the chair and stepped toward her. He was so close now that she had to tilt her head back to look up at him. He was too close and the urge to step back was overwhelming, but she had nowhere to go. The window was to her back and Alex's broad shoulders blocked any escape. She held her breath, waiting for his response.

Without a word Alex lifted his hand and brushed her hair away from her face, allowing the silky strands to sift through his fingers. That lazy smile still played on his lips as he slowly shook his head and made a *tsking* sound. "Celeste Boucher….always so suspicious."

His eyes locked on hers and she couldn't look away. It was as if time stood still. She held her breath. But then he stepped back and the spell was broken. She closed her eyes and took a deep breath, willing her body to relax. When she opened them again Alex was standing a few feet away, his back to her.

"I'm sorry I lied to you," he said softly. Celeste had to concentrate to hear his words and took a step towards him. "I was out this morning. I had a business meeting."

Confused Celeste asked, "then why didn't you just say that? Why did you lie about where you were?"

This time when Alex spoke he turned to face her. "Because I didn't want to have to explain what the meeting was about." A shy smile ticked at the corner of his mouth and he ducked his head. He suddenly became fascinated with the pattern in the rug, running the toe of his shoe across it.

Celeste was taken aback by this. Alex always appeared to be strong and fearless. She never expected to see this side of him. Unconsciously she took another step towards him.

"I was meeting with some city council members regarding a new women's shelter that is in the works. I agreed to donate a large sum of money to fund the project and I have been meeting with them to discuss the plans."

As Alex explained, Celeste was surprised to find herself believing him. She knew that he was a big contributor to many charities. And, now that she thought about it, those men did look vaguely familiar. Though local politics was not her area of expertise she did recall that she had seen them before at various city functions.

"Why didn't you just tell me the truth from the very beginning?" As the words left her lips the answer immediately became clear to her. Alex didn't want anyone to know. It was quite obvious by his actions, and reluctance to tell her, that he wanted to keep his good deeds quiet. But why?

Alex shrugged his shoulders. "I'm a vampire remember? I don't like to draw too much attention to myself, so I tend to keep these things low key."

Of course, she thought. How could she have forgotten? Sometimes he acted so…normal that she completely forgot that he wasn't. That he was far from normal in fact.

Her heart warmed at his kind actions. His selflessness. All of her doubts about him seemed to be erased instantly. Though she still had her qualms about his actions with the young woman, she pushed them aside. There would be time to talk about that later after she spoke to the woman and found out what was really going on.

For now, though, Celeste remained silent. Going to him she stood up on her tiptoes and softly pressed her lips to his.

Alex pulled back slightly and looked deep into her eyes. "So, does this mean that you believe me?" he asked.

Celeste could see the concern clouding his blue eyes. Smiling reassuringly she nodded, pulling his head down so that their lips could meet once again.

CHAPTER 25

Celeste awoke slowly. A satisfied smile languidly spreading across her face. Slowly opening her eyes she was surprised to find the room cast in long shadows. The bright afternoon sunlight had dimmed to a faint orange glow. She couldn't believe that they had wasted half the day in bed, though she wasn't complaining.

Rolling over she reached for Alex, but found the bed beside her empty and cold. Sitting up she looked around the room, but found that it too was empty. *Where is he?*

Slipping from bed she grabbed her robe and shoved her arms into the sleeves as she made her way to the bedroom door. Stepping out into the living room she found the room cast in the amber glow of a handful of candles placed about the room.

Alex was by the sofa lighting two more candles that were placed on the coffee table. A vase of red roses graced the center of the table. As she emerged from the bedroom he straightened and smiled. "Hello sleepyhead," he said, the words teasing yet gentle.

Celeste looked about the room, stunned by Alex's romantic gesture. "What's all this?"

Walking towards her Alex stopped, dropped a quick kiss on the top of her head, than continued towards the kitchenette. "I thought you might be hungry when you woke up." He gave her a heated stare, both of them remembering their earlier lovemaking. "So, while you were napping I stepped out and picked us up some dinner." Holding up two plates he walked back over to the coffee table and set them down, then gestured towards the sofa. "Sit," he said, waiting until she had done so before settling down beside her.

Celeste hadn't realized how hungry she was until she looked down at the pizza before her. The aroma wafting up to fill her senses and cause her stomach to growl softly. She quickly dug in.

"I hope that pizza is okay. I didn't want to go too far and the pizza place around the corner was closest."

"Mmm. Delicious," she said around a mouthful of dough and cheese. Swallowing she looked at him and smiled, "it's perfect."

She watched as he picked up his own piece and took a bite, raising a questioning brow as he did so. He shrugged in response. Laughing, she settled back on the sofa, resting the plate on her crossed legs.

They enjoyed their meal in comfortable silence. When they finished Alex stood, grabbing up both their plates. "Another piece?" he asked as he walked away.

"Yes, please." A moment later he returned with only one plate this time. Handing it to her he settled back down next to her, this time placing his arm around her shoulders and pulling her closer to him.

"Tell me about your life growing up."

Celeste looked up at him in surprise. She had not expected him to ask her that. "Well, there really isn't much to tell. I had a rather normal childhood."

"Tell me about it anyway," he prompted.

"Okay," she said, shrugging her shoulders. Leaning forward she placed her plate on the coffee table, wiped her fingers with a napkin, and settled back into Alex's arms. "I was actually born here in New Orleans, and we lived here until I was about nine and my stepfather moved us to Boston.

'When I was eight my father died in a car accident leaving my mother, who was pregnant with my sister, and me on our own."

Alex lifted her chin and looked deep into her eyes, "I am so sorry, Celeste."

She could see the genuine concern in his blue eyes and smiled up at him reassuringly. "Thank you, but it was a long time ago. It's okay." She lightly patted his cheek then snuggled closer and continued her story. "My mother did her best, but it was just too hard for her. Thankfully, my father's best friend, Jim, was there to help us. He started stopping by just to check on us. Then whenever something needed to be fixed Jim was there. It finally got to the point where he just seemed to be there all the time, but neither my mother nor I really minded. I know she liked having a man around the house again, and he could actually get her to laugh even after everything that had happened. As for myself, Jim always made time for me, even suffering through tea parties and an endless parade of Barbie dolls." She smiled at the memory. "So, when he asked my mother to marry him it wasn't really a surprise, and neither was my mother's answer.'

'They married not long after my sister was born, and that was when we learned that we would have to move. Jim's company was transferring him to Boston, so we packed up and left New Orleans. I think that for my mother it was a relief. It gave her the opportunity to leave the past behind and start over. For me, though, it was bittersweet. The thought of moving to a new city was thrilling, but it was also sad to leave the only life I had known behind."

She fell silent and Alex gave her a moment to reflect as the memories came flooding back. Finally he said, "tell me about Boston."

Sighing she said, "Boston was great. I grew up with a loving family, nice house, and everything I could ever want. Except a pony." She let out a laugh at the last, which brought a smile to Alex's face. "There really isn't much else to say."

Alex seemed to give this some thought, "so, after college you came back here?"

"Yep."

"Why?" he asked.

"As I said, Boston was great, but New Orleans always held a place in my heart. When I graduated I could have stayed in Boston, there were plenty of newspapers that I could have worked for there, but the need to come back here was just too great. So, I packed up everything, said goodbye to my family, and headed on down here." As an afterthought she added, "I didn't even have a job lined up. But, thankfully, I got the first job I interviewed for and have been there ever since."

After a few minutes of silence Celeste looked up at Alex. He was staring off across the room seeming to mull over everything she had told him. As if sensing her eyes on him he looked down at her and smiled. "You're an amazing woman Celeste Boucher," he said, caressing her cheek.

Celeste caught her breath, touched by his sincere words. As his fingers played against her skin she closed her eyes and reveled in the pleasure he offered.

As his fingers trailed down her neck and played along the collar of her robe, Celeste all but purred and leaned into his touch. When those fingers slipped beneath the robe to caress one plump breast she caught her breath, the pleasure intensifying.

She felt Alex shift, then felt his lips brush against her temple. "I don't know about you sweetheart, but I think it just might be time to go back to bed."

Alex rose to his feet, sweeping Celeste up in his arms as he did so. Wrapping her arms around him she nuzzled his neck and said, "I think your right."

CHAPTER 26

"Good morning."

Celeste opened her eyes and looked up at Alex, who was leaning over her. Smiling she stretched. "Good morning to you too."

"I thought that you might appreciate this."

Celeste propped herself up in bed and looked down at the plate in his hand. She let out a squeal of delight. "An omelet." Leaning forward she gave him a quick peck on the cheek. "Thank you."

Taking the plate from him she quickly took a bite. Her eyes widened in surprise. "Wow! This really is good."

"I told you it was," he said matter-of-factly. "You don't have to seem so surprised." He chuckled and tapped the tip of her nose with his finger as he settled more comfortably on the bed beside her. "What's the plan for today? My schedule is free, so I'm all yours." Walking his fingers up her thigh he said with a sultry voice, "we could spend the day in bed."

Swatting his hand away, she giggled. "As tempting as that sounds….it seems like such a beautiful day. I think that I'd like to actually get out and enjoy it." Swallowing the last bite of her omelet Celeste turned and placed the empty plate on the night table. Snuggling back up to Alex she said, "I don't have any plans myself so….." Her eyes widened and she gasped. "Oh, no. Joe and Kathy."

Groaning she flopped onto her back. Alex looked down at her with a puzzled expression. "Joe and Kathy?"

"Joe is my boss," she explained. "He and his wife Kathy invited us to dinner tonight and I already agreed to be there."

"Us?"

Celeste kicked herself mentally. Had she just said *us*? She hadn't meant to. She hadn't wanted to tell Alex about dinner tonight because she wasn't sure if she wanted to bring him. Things were moving really fast here, and she just wasn't sure what to make of their relationship at this point. She just didn't want to introduce him to Joe and Kathy until she had sorted things out. Until she understood how she really felt about him. Now it was too late.

Slowly she said, "yes…I happened to mention you to Joe, and so he invited you to come as well."

"You mentioned me?" Surprise and amusement shone in his eyes.

"Yes. Well, I mentioned that you were helping me with my story."

"That's all."

Narrowing her eyes she glared at him. "Yes. That's

all"

Sighing Alex lay back and looked up at the ceiling. "Do you want me there?"

There was a moment of silence then Celeste whispered softly, "yes." She heard Alex let out the breath he had apparently been holding. Did it mean that much to him that she wanted him there? "Do you want to come?"

Rolling to face her, Alex looked deeply into her eyes. "These people are very important to you." It wasn't a question. "It would be an honor."

Her eyes welled up and, leaning forward, she bridged the few inches that separated them and kissed him softly, then jumped off the bed. Heading for the closet she threw over her shoulder, "now that that's settled, I'm in the mood for a good run. What do you say?"

It was Alex's turn to groan this time. "Let me get dressed," he heaved on a sigh.

Celeste flashed him a brilliant smile as she pulled out a fresh pair of shorts and a shirt.

CHAPTER 27

After their morning run, they returned to Celeste's apartment for a long, steamy shower. Then they headed to Alex's house so he could get a fresh change of clothes. By then it was noon and Alex insisted on treating Celeste to lunch.

While talking and laughing over Po' Boys, Celeste couldn't help but marvel at the fact that it felt like they were a normal couple. Well, almost. It was so easy to forget that Alex wasn't just an ordinary guy, but a vampire. That thought sobered her up a little.

With their sandwiches long since gone, Celeste finished off the last of her coffee and placed the cup back on the saucer. "I'd like to head over to Joe's soon. I know dinner isn't for another few hours, but I always like to get there in the early afternoon. I usually help Kathy prepare dinner and I know she enjoys the company." Looking a little sheepish she added, "I hope you don't mind."

"Not at all."

"You may regret that," she said with a wry smile. At

his razed brow she explained, "just wait until Joe has you cornered and he's drilling you about your intentions. He tends to think of me as a daughter and he can be a little protective at times."

"Oh, well in that case…." he paused and Celeste held her breath. "We better get going then. Don't want to keep them waiting."

Celeste released the breath on a shaky laugh. Relaxing, she took the hand he offered her and, lacing her fingers with his, they headed off to Joe's.

***

"He's very handsome."

Celeste and Kathy were in the kitchen preparing dinner. Celeste was slicing tomatoes for the salad as Kathy prepared the steaks for the grill.

Looking up, Celeste spied Alex and Joe outside in the shade of a big old oak tree. They had started up the grill and were now standing around with a couple of beers in their hands. They were talking about god knows what, but appeared to be enjoying themselves.

"He sure is." She said with a smile.

Kathy gave her a knowing look and wiped her hands on her apron. "He seems very nice too." She gave Celeste a quick squeeze. "You did good" Picking up the plate,

Kathy headed out the door, Celeste following behind with the salad. Tears pricked her eyes. Kathy was like a second mother to Celeste, and her approval meant the world to her.

"Here they are boys," Kathy called out, handing the plate over to Joe. "It's all up to you now, sweetie."

Joe took the plate and gave her a quick peck on the cheek. "The grill's all fired up and waiting."

Celeste watched the interaction between Joe and Kathy with envy, hoping that one day she could have what they had. Wondered if it was even possible. Relationships could be so much work, but they made it look so easy.

"They are really good people." Alex had come up behind her and wrapped his arms around her waist, leaning his cheek against her hair.

"Yeah. They are the best," Celeste said as she covered his hands with hers. Giving them a gentle squeeze, she slipped from his embrace. Turning she gave him a mischievous grin. "I need to help Kathy finish up in the kitchen before those steaks are done." She lightly pat his cheek and hurried back inside. There she found Kathy removing plates from the cupboard and placing them on a tray already laden with silverware, glasses, and a pitcher of lemonade. Celeste hurried over. "Here. Let me get that," she said, taking the tray from Kathy.

"Thank you, dear." Kathy gave her a warm smile, then turned back to the counter to scoop up the bowl of homemade potato salad that she had prepared earlier.

Both women walked back outside and placed everything on the patio table.

"Steaks are done," Joe declared as he placed the

platter in the center of the table. "Bon appetite."

They all took their seats. "Everything looks delicious," Alex said, spooning a helping of the potato salad on his plate. Celeste looked at him and gave him a knowing and grateful smile. She knew that the last thing he wanted to eat was the meal before him.

They all dug in. The conversation was light and before long their plates were empty. "Let me just clean all of this up," Kathy said as she started scooping up the plates and placing them back on the tray.

"Let me." Alex quickly rose and took the plates from Kathy. He loaded them onto the tray along with the dirty utensils and bowls.

"Thank you dear." Alex flashed Kathy that million watt smile and grabbed up the tray to carry into the kitchen. Celeste followed behind.

As Alex placed everything in the sink, Celeste came up behind him and slipped her arms around his waist giving him a gentle squeeze. "Thank you."

Alex turned and cupped her face with his hands. "No thanks are needed. I really enjoyed myself today. Spending time with you, Joe, and Kathy was great. They are so welcoming. They invited me, a stranger, into their home and made me feel like I belong here. It's been awhile since I've felt part of a family."

The sincerity and sadness in his voice brought tears to her eyes. Swallowing hard around the lump in her throat she said, "well, I'm so glad you came with me. I've had a really great time with you today too. It was nice to just forget about everything and enjoy ourselves a little." She sighed and picked up the dishtowel. "But we do need to get back to work tonight." Tossing the towel at him she added, "after we do these dishes."

Turning the faucet on, she smiled at him over her shoulder. "I'll wash and you dry."

CHAPTER 28

After the dishes had been washed, dried, and put away, Celeste and Alex said their goodbyes. As she gave Joe a hug he whispered in her ear, "he seems like a good man. I wish you luck, sweetheart." Tears threatened once more and Celeste quickly blinked them away.

They waved goodbye one last time as they got into Alex's car, and headed back to Celeste's apartment. There they quickly changed and headed back out to The Lair. As the night was warm and pleasant they decided to walk to the club, hand in hand.

Upon arriving, they once again found it crowded and they had to push their way through the throng of people to get to the bar. Alex ordered them drinks and Celeste settled on the only barstool that was unoccupied.

"Thank you," she said as Alex handed her a glass of wine. She took a sip and watched as he took a swig of his beer. "Now what?"

"We wait."

"Wait? Why don't we just go looking for Demitri?"

"As much as I would like to, it looks as if they have beefed up their security over the last few days. If we go snooping around they will toss us out in a heartbeat". He shook his head. "No, we stay here and wait. The night is still young. Demitri is bound to show his face eventually." Begrudgingly, Celeste accepted what he said and took another sip from her glass.

She looked around the room, studying the people and tapping her foot along to the music, but after about an hour she started to get bored. She glanced at Alex who was scanning the club for any sign of Demitri. On full alert. She had tried earlier to engage him in some conversation, but he had been too distracted so she just gave up. Finally, not being able to sit there any longer, Celeste stood. "I'm going to the ladies room."

Alex tore his gaze from the crowed and looked at her. He frowned and said, "Ok. I'll take you."

Celeste rolled her eyes. "I don't need a chaperone. I can use the restroom all by myself."

Alex ignored her and took her arm.

"Alex. This isn't necessary. I-" Alex's grip tightened on her arm and his entire body stiffened. "What's wrong?"

"Stay here. Do not move."

"What is going on?" Celeste turned and saw a tall, well dress man standing by the curtains beside the stage. He was staring at them. A shiver ran up her spine as his cold eyes focused on her. "Is that Demitri?"

Alex didn't respond. Instead, he took off, forcing his way through the crowd towards the man and leaving Celeste standing there stunned.

***

It took Alex only seconds to make it to the curtained doorway, but Demitri was already gone. Throwing the drapes back he spied a figure rounding the corner at the end of the hall. He pursued, crashing through the exit door and out into the night.

Catching sight of a man darting down the alley he followed. "Dimitri," he shouted. The figure stopped and slowly turned.

"Ah, Alexandru Razvan, as I live and breathe." He offered up a wry smile and opened his arms wide in welcome. "To what do I owe this visit?"

Alex seethed, but kept his voice calm. "You know exactly what I'm doing here."

"I see. You heard about the opening of my new club and wanted to wish me luck."

"I'm here about those girls."

"Girls?" Dimitri feigned thought, tapping a finger against his lips. "I don't seem to recall any particular girls. Could you be more specific?"

Alex took a step towards Dimitri. "The girls who recently went missing?"

"Oh, yes. I heard about that on the news." He shook

his head and tsked. "So sad."

"I'm sure you're heartbroken," Alex said sarcastically. Dimitri only smiled. "Where are they Dimitri?"

Surprised, Dimitri said, "I haven't the faintest idea."

"Cut the act, Dimitri. I know you killed those girls and discarded them like garbage. That is your MO."

Dimitri dropped the pretense. "They were only humans." He all but spit the words out. "There are billions of them in this world, what does it matter if a few go missing?"

The anger that had been simmering within Alex threatened to boil over. "It's wrong and you know it."

"*No*, it's not. For us it's life. It's the way things are supposed to be." Dimitri's smile turned sinister and pure evil burned in his eyes. "Natural selection, Alex. We are just higher on the food chain."

Alex fisted his hands at his sides. "I won't let you get away with this. You will answer for what you've done."

Dimitri shook his head. "It's such a shame, really, that you've become weak. Just like your maker." He made a face. "Feeling sorry for the poor humans." He fixed Alex with a knowing stare. "And falling in love with them."

The tight rein he had on his self-control snapped and Alex lunged at Dimitri, fangs bared. Grabbing him by the shirt Alex slammed him into the brick wall of the club.

Dimitri bared his fangs as well then laughed, knowing that his suspicions had right and he had hit his mark. "Temper, temper." Reaching up he grabbed Alex's hands.

"She's a beautiful woman. Does she know what you really are?"

Alex's grip tightened and he growled. "I'll-"

"Alex!"

Alex's head snapped up at the sound of Celeste's voice. With his attentions elsewhere, Dimitri took advantage and forced Alex away, flinging him across the alley to smack against the opposite wall and fall to the ground. Once free Dimitri looked at Celeste and sneered.

CHAPTER 29

Celeste had remained rooted to the spot where Alex had left her, staring at the curtain he had disappeared behind. But, after looking around the room and noticing a few people leering at her, practically salivating, unease had crept up her spine. She had to get out of there.

Making up her mind, she had started for the door, but came up short. Walking towards her was the girl. Her source.

The girl had spotted Celeste and froze. They had stood there a moment, staring at each other, then the girl had quickly turned and rushed out the door. Celeste had followed.

Unfortunately, she had quickly lost the girl in the crowd of people that filled the street. Frustrated, and still worried about Alex, she had turned back toward the club. But, from the corner of her eye she saw a shadow move in the ally. The same alley she had been in the night she met Alex.

Throwing caution to the wind she had headed in that

direction. Something she couldn't explain had drawn her forward almost against her will.

When she had rounded the corner her eyes were drawn immediately to the two figures locked together near the far end of the alley. Squinting in an effort to get a better look in the dim lighting she had moved slowly closer and realized that it was Alex and most probably Dimitri.

Demitri was on the ground and Alex was over him, pinning him down. Instinctively she had called out to Alex. Unfortunately, that was the wrong thing to do, though, as her distraction gave Dimitri the upper hand and he flung Alex away from him as if he were a rag doll.

When Dimitri turned his attentions on Celeste, goosebumps rose on her flesh and she tried to hold back the chill that ran through her body at the look that he gave her. Frozen in place, she watched as he casually straightened his clothing, and then, in the blink on an eye, vanished.

Realizing that she was standing there like an idiot, Celeste forced herself to move and quickly went to Alex's side. She crouched down beside him just as he pushed himself to a seated position.

Concern pinched her features and she allowed her eyes to scan over him. "Are you alright?"

"I'm fine," he snapped, forcefully pushing her hand away. Rising to his feet he dusted off his clothes. "I had him. I had him then you came and-" He swore under his breath.

Celeste watched as he paced back and forth. This was the first time that she had seen him angry and unease settled over her. He had been so patient and easy going up to this point that she hadn't even considered the fact that he might have a temper. That there might be a darker side to him.

She didn't know what to say so she simply said, "I'm sorry."

Alex stopped and looked at her. "Sorry?" He advanced. He looked so menacing that for a moment fear took hold and she stepped back. Anger rolled off of him and he seemed to ignore her reaction, not stopping until they were toe to toe. "You're *sorry*?" he boomed.

Shaking off her momentary fear Celeste stood her ground, anger bolstering her courage. *How dare he?* She made a mistake. People do. But she said she was sorry. What more could he want? "Yes, I'm sorry. I made a mistake. Happy?"

"No, I am not happy. Do you have any idea what you've done?" His voice rose. "I have been searching for Dimitri for so long and I had him right in my grasp." He looked down at his hands. His voice lowered to almost a whisper. "And once again he slipped away." Instantly the anger seemed to drain away and regret took its place. Forcing a hand through his hair he turned away from her and took a few steps. Celeste watched his shoulders rise and fall as he took a deep, calming breath. Then he said in a more even tone, "I thought I told you to stay put!"

He looked defeated, and the anger that had filled her only a moment before faded away. "You did, and I tried," she shook her head even though she knew he couldn't see, "you were right about that place, it is really creepy and the people in there kept staring at me like I was dinner or something." She shook her head again realizing she had gotten off track. "But the reason I left is because of a girl. My contact. When she saw me she spooked and ran. I went after her, but I lost her in the street. That's when I noticed you and Dimitri here, in the alley."

Celeste studied his back, waiting for a reaction. Nothing. Shame filled her. With his last words she had heard the regret in his voice. She knew that she was the cause of it, and nothing she said would change that.

She should have been more understanding. After all, he had every right to be mad at her. She had promised him that she would stay put and she didn't, even though she had a good reason. Not only that, but she had walked into a dangerous situation making things worse.

Tentatively she placed a hand on his shoulder and squeezed, trying to convey how she felt. "I really am sorry."

"I know." Sighing, he continued to stare at the wall opposite them. "You could have been hurt Celeste. He could have come after you." Taking her hand from his shoulder he held onto it as he turned to face her. As he looked deep into her eyes she could see concern and...fear? What could he possibly be afraid of? "He knows about us. It won't take him long now to find out who you are, and he will come after you."

"Oh." She knew she couldn't hide the worry and uncertainty in her eyes, but despite it she lifted her chin in that stubborn way of hers and said, "well he can try, but he has to get past you first. And, if I had to choose, I'd put my money on you any day."

Alex smiled. Looking down at her hand he turned it over and brought it to his lips, brushing a light kiss across her palm. "You certainly do know how to boost a man's ego, but..." his smile disappeared. "This is serious Celeste. Dimitri is very dangerous. He just admitted to killing those girls and didn't even blink an eye."

She closed her eyes. "I knew it. I knew they were dead." Her heart sank to the pit of her stomach. *Those poor girls.* She thought of their families and she fought the urge to cry. She knew that they were still holding out hope that their daughters would come home safe, but now those hopes were dashed. *They will be devastated.*

"We have to go now." Pulling her out of the alley Alex briefly glanced down at her shoes and asked, "Can you keep up in those or will I have to carry you?"

"Don't worry I can keep up."

They rushed down the street towards her apartment, her heels clicking frantically against the pavement. By the time they reached his car she could hardly catch her breath. When he open the door and pushed her down into the seat she asked, "Where are we going? My apartment is right here."

Alex slammed the door and rounded the hood. Getting in beside her he revved the engine and pulled out into the street, tires squealing as he did so. "We can't go back there. I told you that it won't be long before Dimitri learns your name, and when he does he will go right to your apartment looking for you." He turned the wheel sharply and Celeste grabbed the door handle in order to stop from sliding off the seat and landing in his lap. "We are going to my house. I'll be able to better protect you there."

Celeste looked out the windshield and saw two women up ahead, about to cross the street. As they flew towards them she clamped her eyes shut and braced herself. Waiting for the sickening thud that she knew was inevitable. But nothing happened. Cracking one eye she saw the world passing by in a blur, but no sign of the women. Craning her head around, she saw them safely on the opposite side of the street.

Breathing a sigh of relief she looked at Alex and asked, "is it necessary to go so fast? These streets are teeming with people. It's way too dangerous to be going this fast."

***

Alex ignored her. As he sped through a red light he heard her gasp and smiled to himself. He had been driving since Ford issued the first Model A at the turn of the twentieth century, and he was damn good at it. Celeste, however, didn't seem to have as much confidence in his abilities.

Only when they were within a couple of blocks of his house did Alex let up on the gas, and by the time they turned into the driveway he had slowed the car to a crawl. Parking in the garage he cut the engine and jumped out, opening Celeste's door within a heartbeat. "Let's get you inside," he said looking around suspiciously.

As they rounded the house, Alex checked his pace. Something wasn't right. As they got closer and closer the feeling became stronger. He realized that they weren't alone.

"Stay put," he said to Celeste as he crept up the steps. Cautiously he opened the door.

The intruder had to be someone he knew. There was no way that it was Dimitri. Alex had never invited Dimitri into his home before. *Who are you?*

He stepped through the doorway and searched the darkness around him. The house was deathly quiet, expect for the sound of even breathing. A sound that could be heard by no human, but only a vampire. A sound that was coming closer.

Sensing the presence behind him, Alex spun around and had the intruder up against the wall in the blink of an eye. His fangs were drawn in readiness of the confrontation.

"I've never seen you so jumpy before, Alex." The voice was calm, a touch of amusement evident.

Alex stared into stormy grey eyes. "Sam? What the hell are you doing here?" Alex released his friend and stepped back.

"Alex?" Celeste poked her head around the door and her gaze fell on the stranger. She eyed him warily.

Alex waved her in. "It's alright. This is Sam. A friend of mine and my boss." Turning to Sam he said, "Sam, meet Celeste."

"Ah, your Alex's human. I've heard so much about you."

Celest's chin came up and she gave him a hard look. "I'm not Alex's. I don't belong to anyone."

Alex smiled and Sam let out a laugh. Glancing at Alex, Sam said, "she's spunky," then turned his attentions back to Celeste. "I'm charmed madam," He took her hand and bent over it to place a brief kiss across her knuckles.

CHAPTER 30

Celeste eyed the man before her. Standing a few inches taller than Alex, he had sharper features and intriguing grey eyes. He seemed pleasant enough and gentlemanly. *He's a friend of Alex's so he must be okay.* She relaxed a little and smiled back at him. "It's nice to meet you too."

"So, what have I missed?" Sam directed the question at Alex.

Alex looked away and hit the light switch. "How about we go in and take a seat?"

Celeste noted the reluctance in Alex before he turned his back to them, and without waiting for a response from either of them he walked into the living room, expecting them to follow.

They did. Celeste took a seat on the sofa and Sam settled into an armchair. Walking over to the fireplace Alex braced his hands against it, staring at them through the mirror over the mantle. "I made some headway today. Found out some information about that club that I had told you about, The Lair." Sam nodded and waited, but

Alex didn't continue.

"We just came back from there," Celeste added.

"Really? Both of you, huh?" Sam directed his question to Celeste, but kept his eyes pinned on Alex's in the mirror.

Oblivious to the silent communication between the two men Celeste continued, "Oh, yeah. We've been working together to try and get this Dimitri guy. He's the one who owns The Lair, and the one who is behind the disappearances of those girls." She paused to take a breath. "Anyway, we went there tonight to catch him, and Alex did, but I screwed things up and he got away."

"Sounds like you had an interesting night." Sam flashed her a smile, but the look in his eyes told her that he was not happy. She looked at Alex, who looked equally unhappy, and unease crept up her spine.

The tension between both men filled the room and a heavy silence enveloped them. She thought about telling him about the girl, but decided that now was probably not the right time. *Damn.* Her mouth was always getting her into trouble. And now, it would seem, her mouth was getting Alex in to trouble too. She really needed to learn to keep it shut.

Her discomfort grew and she finally said, "I, uh, need to use the ladies room." She stood up and looked at Alex, trying to convey how much she was sorry.

"You can use the one upstairs. First door on the left." Celeste nodded and left the room.

***

As soon as Celeste was out of earshot, Sam turned on Alex, "What the hell were you thinking?"

Alex shook his head. "I know...I know. I screwed up."

"And now you have this human involved in all this."

Alex cringed. "Believe me, there's no way I can forget."

Sam leaned back in his chair and studied Alex. "You've slept with her haven't you?" Alex didn't respond and Sam shook his head. "I don't get it, Alex. You are one of the best Guardians that I've ever worked with, how did you let this happen?"

Alex pushed away from the fireplace and sank down onto the sofa. Sam was right. He wasn't conceited by any means, but he had to admit that he was damn good at what he did. His work was his life. It had been for longer then he cared to admit, and he had never let his personal life-not that he really had one-interfere. Until now that was. "I keep asking myself that same question."

"You need to fix this. The smart thing to do would be to end things with Celeste before they get serious, and finish your job."

Unable to look Sam in the eye, Alex hung his head and said, "it's not that simple, Sam"

Sam's eyes narrowed on Alex. "You've fallen in love

with her?"

At that, Alex's head shot up and his eyes flew to Sam's. "What? No. My god, Sam, we've only known each other a few days."

"But you do care about her." It was a statement, not a question.

"I don't want to see her get hurt, if that's what you mean."

"Either way, you need to figure this out fast before someone else goes missing. Before that someone ends up being Celeste."

CHAPTER 31

"Maybe I should stick around. You look like you could use all the help you can get." Celeste could just make out Sam's words as she neared the living room. *He's not yelling, so I guess he's not that mad. Maybe I should just stay out here and give them a few more minutes....*

"You can stop lurking outside the door and come in now, Celeste."

Startled, she jumped at the sound of Alex's voice. *God, that man is so frustrating.* "I was not lurking," she said as she breezed into the room. "I just came down the stairs and was about to walk in." She sat down next to Alex-who was now seated on the sofa-and glared at him, then turned a smile on Sam. "So, Sam, do you plan on staying?"

He chuckled, "I was just telling Alex that I should stay for a while and help you two out."

"Oh." She placed a hand on Alex's knee and looked at him. "That's nice isn't it?"

"Yeah, real nice," he mumbled.

Celeste looked up to find Sam studying both of them intently. Holding her questioning glance a moment, he smiled warmly then looked down at his watch. Faking a yawn he said, "well, it's been a long night and it will be dawn before too long. I can certainly use some sleep."

"You're right," Alex said, standing up. "We could all use some sleep. You can use the same room you had last time, if that's alright with you."

"That's fine. Thanks." Looking at Celeste, Sam said, "Goodnight."

"Goodnight."

Both she and Alex watched Sam walk out of the room. When he was gone Alex looked down at her. "What do you say?" he said as he held a hand out to her.

Celeste looked up into his eyes. There was no mistaking the look of desire that burned there and her pulse quickened. Feeling a sudden urge to be in his arms she slipped her hand in his and rose, following him up the stairs.

***

Sam had quickly gone up to his room and shut the door. A moment later he heard the click of a door closing down the hall, and the soft murmur of voices, one female and one male. Shaking his head he lay down on the bed, fully clothed.

He had studied the interaction between Alex and Celeste intently, and by the looks of things-and judging by the sounds that were coming from down the hall at that moment-he knew that Alex was fighting a losing battle. It was clear that he was falling for this woman, whether he liked it or not, and the thought worried Sam.

He didn't know many vampire and human couples, but he did know that things were definitely more complicated for them. And things didn't always work out. Sam knew that Alex had experienced this first hand, and he didn't want to see history repeat itself for his old friend.

He just hoped, for Alex's sake, that he was wrong and they could make it work. Besides, times had changed. People were a lot more open minded now than they had been in the past. Maybe Celeste could accept Alex for who he was. What he was. After all, Alex deserved a little happiness.

***

"What do you want?"

"I have that information you wanted."

"Give it to me." Dimitri grabbed the sheet of paper from Roman's hand and read it over. Sitting back in his chair, he murmured, "Celeste Boucher. Why does that name sound familiar?"

"She's a reporter for a local paper. She's written a couple of articles about those girls."

"Ah, yes. I did enjoy those pieces she wrote. They were very moving." He laughed and picked up his drink, allowing the paper to fall from his hand and float down to the table. "So, it appears as though Alexandru has gotten himself involved with the little reporter. Tsk. Tsk." A cold smile curled his lips. "He will certainly regret that decision."

"What's the plan then?"

Dimitri looked up at Roman. "Will you stop hovering? I really cannot stand that."

Roman quickly took a seat across from Dimitri. "What do you want me to do?"

"Well…" Dimitri gave it some thought. "I believe that we should pay Miss Boucher a visit." Setting down his glass, he rose and began to pace. "If I know Alexandru," his face scrunched up with contempt as he said the words. "He has got it in his head that he must protect this creature. My bet is that he has her secreted in that mausoleum he calls a house."

"Then how are we supposed to get her?"

"Really, Roman, is there a brain in that head of yours?" Dimitri rolled his eyes, then explained slowly so that Roman would understand, "you go to Alexandru's house with a couple of those humans that have worked for us before, and they can grab the girl. In the meantime, I will pay a little visit to her apartment."

"Why?"

Dimitri clenched his teeth and prayed for patience. It was a good thing that Roman was so loyal or he would have gotten rid of him long ago.

He finally answered, responding as if he were explaining things to a small child. "Because, as I said before, I know Alexandru. I know that he will have expected me to find out about Miss Boucher, and will expect me to show up there. I certainly do not want to disappoint him. And, also, it will distract him long enough for you to get the girl."

"When do you plan for this to take place?"

"We will post someone outside the house to keep an eye on things. My guess is that they will be pretty busy tomorrow, after they find my little present, and by tomorrow evening Alex should be more than ready for me."

Roman rose. As he made his way to the door Dimitri stopped him with a hand to his arm. "Speaking of presents. Have you taken care of it?"

"I'm leaving now."

"Good. Good." Roman left and Dimitri picked the paper up from the table, reading the name and address once more. "Celeste Boucher, I can't wait until we meet again."

CHAPTER 32

He stopped and listened. Nothing. The usual sounds of the night were silent. Something was wrong.

As he neared the village he saw the lone light shining in Dr. Stefan Patrascu's window. The doctor should have been in bed by now, which meant that someone must be sick. He moved closer and glimpsed shadows moving across the wall. They appeared to be locked together as if in battle.

He had to get to the doctor, but he stopped. Something just wasn't right. The smell of blood and death hit him, and he looked around, finally aware of the carnage around him. There were bodies strewn about the streets. Men, women, and children were laying like broken dolls about the village. The sight sickened him and he stumbled back, fighting the urge to scream out in anger.

Dr. Patrascu! He had to get to him. Carefully stepping over the bodies he made his way to the doctor's house and peered in the window. The sight before him filled him with rage.

It was clear that there had been a fight. Tables and chairs were upended, and books were strewn about the room. The doctor's precious tools littered the floor. The doctor, himself, was in the middle of the room on his knees, a defiant look etched into his features. Standing over him, with his back to the window, was a man, sword in hand. In one quick stroke the man brought the sword down, severing the doctor's head.

"No!" The scream was ripped from his throat. In shock he watched as the man turned to face him. Dimitri. *The doctor's friend. Why?*

He jumped back as the door flew open and Dimitri was upon him, sword in hand. Dimitri raised the sword and he stumbled backwards, tripped, and fell. The sword was at his throat, pinning him to the ground. "I should kill you where you lay." Dimitri's lips curled into a cold, evil sneer. "You are nothing but a young, cowardly fool."

He closed his eyes and waited for the end to come. It did not. When he opened his eyes Dimitri was gone. Rising to his feet he ran into the house then dropped to his knees beside the pile of ash on the floor. All that was left of his friend, Dr. Stefan Patrascu.

Alex awoke with a start and bolted up in bed. The dream had been so vivid it was like he had been there all over again.

Running shaky fingers across his face and back through his hair, he tried to slow his breathing. It had been decades since he had been plagued by that nightmare. He thought he had put it all behind him. Apparently, he was wrong.

He felt Celeste move next to him. A moment later she was sitting up beside him, her warm hand rubbing his back in a comforting gesture. "Are you alright?" He could hear the concern in her voice and was surprised by the feelings it stirred in him. It had been a long time, too long, since anyone had cared enough to sound concerned. He had forgotten how good it felt.

Jennifer Richardson

He bent his head down and brushed a kiss against her forehead. "I'm fine."

Celeste looked at him with doubt, but didn't question him. Instead she placed her head against his arm and gave him a little squeeze. "Do you want to talk about it?"

Alex looked down at the top of her head, hair mussed from their lovemaking earlier. How could he tell this strong, brave woman how much of a coward he had been? How he had failed to save his only friend. "It was nothing. Just a dream." Laying back down he threw an arm over his eyes in an effort to block out the little bit of light that permeated the curtains, and the images still running through his head.

When Celeste didn't lay back down next to him he opened his eyes and stared up at her. Sighing, she said, "Whatever this dream was it clearly upset you. Maybe, if you tell me about it, I can help," then, dipping her head down, she pressed her lips to his chest. Nudging his arm out of the way she buried her head in his shoulder and waited.

Unconsciously, Alex pulled her closer and ran a hand idly over her hair. Emotions warred inside him as he tried to decide whether to tell her or not. He wanted so much to unburden these feelings that the dream had stirred up. He had never really spoken of that night to anyone, and somehow it felt right to tell Celeste. But the thought that she would think less of him for his cowardly actions stopped him.

He knew, deep down, that she would never judge him for what he had done, but that didn't matter. He judged himself and the verdict was guilty. He could never forgive himself and he just couldn't expect Celeste to do so either.

When she raised her head and looked down at him he found it harder and harder to resist. When she gently brushed a lock of hair away from his forehead and whispered, "please," he was completely undone.

Pressing her head back down to his shoulder he took a deep breath and said, "Well, in order to understand the whole story I would have to start at the beginning." He paused, contemplating how much to tell her, and decided that she should know everything. *Let the chips fall where they may*. "When I was a child my father died. My mother was left to raise three young children on her own, which today is hard, but in the seventeenth century was virtually impossible. You see there was no work for women then. My mother scraped by doing mending and laundry, but there was never enough food on the table. Being that I was the oldest at ten years of age, it was decided that I would go to work, but no one wanted to employ a scrawny little boy. Then the town doctor, Stefan Patrascu, took pity on me and put me to work doing odd jobs around his house. I would clean, chop wood, whatever he could think of, and we became good friends.'

'Eventually, when I grew older, I helped assist him with his patients. I had wanted to follow in his footsteps and he was more than willing to teach me. But, then the plague hit. Everyone in the town became afflicted, including me. Stefan did all he could, but the death toll was high. Unfortunately, my mother and sisters did not survive."

Celeste gasped. Raising her head she looked down at him and caressed his cheek. Pain and sadness were evident in her eyes. "I'm so sorry."

He gave her a weak smile. "It was a long time ago, and I have come to terms with it." He turned his head and placed a kiss against her palm then returned her hand to his chest, covering it with his own. When she laid her head back down he continued. "I was in really bad shape myself, and wouldn't have made it through the night. Stefan, kind hearted as he was, couldn't stand to watch his friend die and he turned me. Until then I had never even suspected that he was a vampire.'

'Afterwards, we moved to a different village where he could practice medicine and I could assist him. Things were fine, for a while, then an old friend of Stefan's came to visit. Dimitri."

"Oh, no! You knew Dimitri before this?"

"Unfortunately, yes. But he wasn't evil then, or at least didn't appear to be. Though Stefan mentioned that he had noted a change in Dimitri he didn't seem too concerned by it."

"He should have been."

Frustration laced her voice and Alex smiled. "Well, my dear, hindsight is only twenty-twenty, even for vampires."

"Humph." Her reaction lightened his spirits, which was some feat considering the emotions rocketing through him. It was an amazing feeling knowing that there was someone who responded so passionately to his tragedies. He had never had that before. "Well, he should have driven a stake through Dimitri's heart right then and there, regardless," she said.

Alex shook his head and continued his story. "One night Stefan sent me out to gather some medicinal herbs. When I got back to the village everything was quiet, too quiet, and that's when I noticed the bodies everywhere. Dimitri had slaughtered the villagers, and by the time I made it to Stefan it was too late. I arrived just in time to watch Dimitri behead him."

"Oh, god. You poor thing," she soothed. "What did you do?"

Alex paused. This was the part he didn't want to tell her. Hesitantly he said, "Dimitri saw me in the window and came out, threatening me with the sword. I froze, the point of that sword resting against my throat. I should have fought him, but I was too afraid. For some reason he spared me and disappeared. I've been searching for him ever since."

Celeste pulled away and sat up. "Well, thank god you didn't fight him off or he would have killed you." She sighed, "After all this time you finally found him, and I screwed things up."

Alex cupped her face in his hands. The woman never ceased to surprise him. "It's not your fault. You couldn't possibly have known."

She gave him a halfhearted smile and he kissed her. Laying her back on the bed he covered her body with his, moving against her in slow, sensual movements. "We really should go back to sleep," he said against her lips.

"We should," she agreed, grabbing his hips and thrusting up.

Alex growled deep in his throat and plunged deep inside her, smiling as she cried out his name.

CHAPTER 33

Celeste awoke alone. Rolling onto her back she stared at the ceiling, her thoughts straying to Alex's story. Her heart ached for the pain he had carried all of this time, and still carried.

She was quite surprised that he had even told her. She knew all too well how it felt to loose someone close-she had lost her father after all-and knew it was hard to talk about it.

When she had first asked, she had seen the reluctance in his eyes. She had expected him to refuse, and a surge of anger had shot through her. Why did men always have to act so tough? She would have thought that, being a vampire and living for over three hundred years, he would have learned by now that women didn't think less of a man because he shared his feelings. That it was okay for a man to let down his guard every once in a while and let a woman in.

But she had resisted the urge to argue and had opted for a different tactic. A gentler one. It worked. He opened up to her and she had been shocked and appalled by what Dimitri had done. And by the fact that Alex actually blamed himself for letting Dimitri get away.

Sighing, she threw back the covers and got out of bed. Donning the same clothes she had worn the day before she left the room and descended the stairs.

"Alex?" she called, rounding the staircase and walking into the kitchen. "Are you in-" she stopped short when she saw him standing at the counter, a glass of red liquid in his hand. "Oh, hi."

"I thought you were still sleeping?" Turning he placed the glass in the sink.

"I woke up and you were gone." She stepped up to the counter. "Please, don't let me interrupt. You need to eat…or drink. Whatever you call it."

"I didn't want to make you uncomfortable."

"It doesn't, not really. I mean, it takes some getting used to, but I think I'm starting to. Besides, you must be starving, considering you didn't eat yesterday."

Alex rinsed the glass, dried it, and put it away. "I did actually." He glanced up at her. "Yesterday morning, when we came back here, I had a pint when I went up to shower."

"You keep blood in your bedroom?"

"Yes. I keep a mini-fridge and a microwave up there. I find it's more convenient as I'm usually hungry when I wake up."

"Oh." She didn't know what to say to that so she let it drop. As her stomach was growling she went to the fridge and poked her head in. It was empty expect for a couple of bottles of what appeared to be blood. She didn't want to think about where they had come from.

Alex winced. "Sorry. I don't usually keep food since I rarely eat it. I'll run out and pick up a few things from the store."

"Do you at least have coffee?"

"There should be some in that cabinet." He motioned with his head.

Celeste reached up and found a can on the shelf. Opening the lid she inhaled deeply, a smile slowly spreading across her face. "This should hold me over until you get back."

"Alright, I'll be quick." Dropping a quick kiss on her cheek he left the kitchen. A minute later she heard the front door open then close.

Plugging the coffee pot in, she poured in a scoop, then another for good measure, and filled it with water. Once it was percolating she roamed around the kitchen, curiously peeking into all of the cabinets. Not surprisingly, they were all empty except for a box of stale crackers hiding in a back corner. *Crackers?* They were the last thing she thought she would find.

She did discover a mug though and, after opening a couple of drawers, a spoon. *Just in time* she thought, pouring the dark liquid into the mug. She took a tentative sip and nodded her head in approval. Armed with her trusty cup, she wandered over to the double doors that looked out on the small back garden. Opening them she stepped out onto the patio and breathed in the sweet scent of magnolias. As it was mid-April everything was in bloom and the garden was filled with a riot of colors.

As it was still morning, and the sun hadn't made its way to the back of the house yet, most of the backyard was cast in shade, including the small bistro style table where she planted herself. She sat in silence enjoying the cool breeze and taking in the beauty around her, wondering if Alex did his own gardening. She smiled at the thought. Wouldn't that be a sight, Alex kneeling in the dirt planting Petunias.

"You look like you're enjoying yourself."

Celeste looked up to find Sam standing over her. Pulling out the chair across from her he slipped into it and crossed his arms over his chest as he leaned back. A smile was fixed into place, but there was suspicion in his eyes.

She took a sip from her mug. "Good morning."

"Good morning to you too." He looked around. "Has Alex gone out?"

"He stepped out to pick up some groceries."

Sam nodded his head and they fell into an uncomfortable silence. Celeste averted her eyes, focusing on a nearby potted plant. She could feel Sam staring at her and she nervously took another sip.

His voice finally broke the silence. "He's falling for you."

Celeste's eyes snapped back to his in surprise. "What?"

Sam leaned forward and fixed her with a cold stare. "Alex is my friend. He has been hurt by a human woman before, and I would not like to see that happen again."

Celeste was taken aback by his words. She had not

expected him to be so direct, and she had certainly not expected to find out that Alex had been in love before. She shouldn't have been too surprised though. He was over three hundred years old after all. She wasn't so naïve as to think that he would have been celibate all of that time.

An unexpected stab of jealousy sliced through her heart. *What is wrong with me?* She had no right being jealous. There was nothing serious between her and Alex, was there? They had only known each other a short time. That wasn't long enough to fall in love with someone. Was it?

Celeste looked him in the eye and lifted her chin. "I would never intentionally hurt Alex."

Sam studied her. The conviction in her eyes and the tilt of her chin must have convinced him that she meant what she said, and he nodded his head, the suspicion gone. He relaxed some. "Good," he said, smiling once more. "If you would excuse me I am feeling a bit famished." Rising he disappeared back into the house, leaving Celeste alone with her thoughts.

CHAPTER 34

Alex heard the shower running before he even walked into the bedroom. Crossing to the bathroom, he opened the door just as Celeste turned the water off and was stepping out. Her hair was plastered to her scalp and water glistened on her skin. She looked so beautiful that he couldn't seem to drag his eyes away from the sight of her.

He stood there a moment letting his eyes drink in their fill of her as she reached for the towel and wrapped it around herself. He snapped out of it once she was completely covered and said, "hello." It came out low and a little raspy and he quickly cleared his throat.

She jumped at the sound of his voice and her eyes flew up to meet his. "Will you stop doing that! You're going to give me a heart attack." He laughed and she stomped past him in a huff. "If you don't stop I'm going to have to put a bell around your neck so I can hear you coming."

Smiling, he turned to watch the sway of her hips as she walked away from him, but she stopped abruptly, staring at the suitcase by the door. Looking back at him over her shoulder she raised a questioning brow.

"I stopped by your apartment while I was out. I thought you might like a change of clothes."

An image of him rummaging through her panty drawer must of popped into her head because her cheeks reddened. Picking up the suitcase she turned her back to him-a deliberate attempt to hide her embarrassment-as she placed it on the bed. Flinging it open she seemed surprise to find everything she needed for an extended stay. Even her broken in, worn-out sneakers were tucked in there. "Thank you," she said softly.

***

Celeste had not expected Alex to be so….considerate. She hadn't even thought to ask him to stop by her place and pick up a few things when he had left, but he had taken it upon himself to do so anyway. It was funny how he seemed to know what she wanted or needed. Even when she didn't know herself.

As she went through the suitcase, removing the things she intended to wear, a bit of black lace caught her eye and she pulled it out. Holding the teddy up in front of her, she allowed it to dangle from one finger and looked at him out of the corner of her eye.

He smiled as he slowly walked toward her. Without

taking his eyes off of hers he reached out and slipped the strap from her finger, allowing the material to sift through his hands before it fell to the bed. "I thought that might be useful later."

Celeste's breath caught and she felt that all too familiar jolt of excitement. She waited as he lowered his head and softly brushed his lips across hers. Then, all too quickly, he pulled away. "You better get dressed. Sam's waiting for us down stairs."

It took a moment for her to find her voice. "I'll be right there."

With his smile still in place, Alex trailed his fingers along her jaw and down the curve of her neck, allowing them to rest a moment over her heart. "I'll be waiting." This time, instead of disappearing in a flash, he slowly walked out of the room, turning at the door to give her one more look before he was gone.

CHAPTER 35

Celeste entered the living room to find Alex and Sam deep in conversation. Sinking down onto the sofa beside Alex she looked from one to the other. They were eyeing her intently and she squirmed. "What?"

Alex was the first to answer. "Why don't you tell us about that girl? The one you mentioned last night."

Her eyes narrowed on him. "Why don't you?" Alex didn't even flinch at her words, just continued to hold her gaze. She elaborated. "I saw you with her, then you told me that you never caught up to her. What are you hiding?"

Alex sighed and broke eye contact. "You're right. I have been in contact with her. I lied to you and I am sorry, Celeste."

"Why did you lie? Why didn't you just tell me the truth?"

"At first it was because I didn't want you to get more involved in this than you already were. Then, I just didn't know how to tell you without you getting upset and accusing me of not keeping you in the loop."

"Well, you are right about that," she said as she jumped to her feet and began pacing. "I'm pissed!" She spun around and glared at him. "Do you have any idea what I've been going through? I had no idea what you were up to and what you were trying to hide from me. I thought we were partners in this. You should have told me what you were up to."

"You're right. I'm sorry, but I thought it was for the best."

"What did you learn?"

"What?" He looked at her puzzled.

"What did you learn from her?"

He shook his head. "Not much more than you did I'm sure. She's scared of someone. It has to be Demitri because, whoever it is, she is more scared of them than she is of me. And she knows who and what I am. She wouldn't give me much. Every time I would start questioning her she would clam up. I was even following her for a time, but she didn't lead me anywhere out of the ordinary." He held his hands up in defeat and looked at Celeste. "Now, will you tell us everything you know?"

Celeste sat back down next to him. Taking a deep breath to calm herself, she said, "as you know, she first contacted me shortly after the article on Julie was printed, and told me about The Lair. Since then I've had a few run-ins with her. I've seen her a couple of times now at The Lair and met her once at a coffee shop." She shook her head. "I just don't understand it. I don't know why she keeps going back to the club. She's frightened of that place and has warned me about the danger. She knows that it is a real vampire bar." She looked at Alex. "And you said that she knows what you are. So, why does she keep going back there? None of this makes any sense, and whenever I tried to get more information out of her she got nervous. Scared. She took off every time."

"She was your only contact," Alex said.

"Yes. When I ran into her the first time and she spoke, I recognized her voice. She was the one who called me originally and gave me the information about The Lair."

Alex and Sam looked at each other. A silent understanding passed between them and Celeste looked from one to the other. "Wha-" Before she could finish her question, the cell phone in her pocket buzzed-she had put it on vibrate.

Looking at the call screen she accepted and said, "hey Joe. What's up?" Holding a finger up to indicate that she needed a moment she rose from the sofa and walked over to the window.

"I've got another one for you," Joe said from the other end of the line.

"What?"

"The police found a body. It might be that of one of those girls who went missing."

"Oh, god!" At her exclamation both Alex and Sam looked over at her. She ignored their questioning glances and focused her attentions on Joe's words.

"They found her near Washington Square. I need you to get over there right away. You live right around the corner so you should be able to get there quick enough.

See what you can find out and get back to me. I need something on my desk tonight."

"Alright, I'm on my way there now. Bye." She ended the call and looked at Alex. "They may have found one of the missing girls."

She didn't have to say more. Going by the looks on their faces both Alex and Sam knew, without her having to speak the words, that the girl wasn't found alive.

"I have to get over there now," she said as she hurried out of the room. "I just need to grab my laptop," she threw over her shoulder as she rounded the banister and headed up the stairs.

***

"I'm going with you," Alex called after her as she ran up the stairs, then turned to Sam.

"Don't worry about me I can occupy myself," Sam said. "Besides, I was thinking about canvassing the neighborhood around The Lair. See if I can come up with anything new."

Alex gave him a stiff nod. He knew that Sam was right. Fresh eyes might pick up something that he had missed. But Alex couldn't help but feel like Sam didn't trusted him enough to do his job right.

Ever since Sam had arrived last night he had appeared

wary of the situation. Of Celeste. Did Sam think that she was too much of a distraction? That because of her he couldn't do his job?

He kept his mouth shut though, realizing that now was not the time for petty arguments. Celeste had returned from upstairs and was saying goodbye to Sam before she headed out the door. Mumbling a quick goodbye himself he followed her out.

CHAPTER 36

As Alex's car rounded the corner, flashing lights and yellow crime scene tape came into view. Slowing to a stop, Alex parked about a block away from all the activity and they got out to walk the rest of the way.

A small crowd had gathered on the sidewalk in front of the police block and Celeste skirted it, going straight for the young officer standing off to the side.

"Mike!" Celeste called out to get the officers attention. When he looked her way she gave a little wave, flashed a dazzling smile, and hurried over to him.

"Hey, Celeste. I figured you'd show up sooner or later." Officer Michael Thompson was about thirty, with sandy colored hair, kind green eyes, and a ready smile. With six years on the police force under his belt, some would consider him a veteran.

Celeste had known him for three of those six years. In fact, in her line of work, she knew most of the cops if not by name at least by sight. But out of all of them, Mike was her favorite. He didn't brush her off like most of the others did. He was always pleasant and willing to listen to her questions, answering those that he could and politely refusing to answer those that he couldn't.

The last was the reason why Celeste had been relieved to see him standing there. She knew that he would truthfully inform her as much as he could. She also knew that he would give her the scoop over any other reporters who happened to be milling about.

"Yep. I'm nothing if not predictable." As Alex came up alongside her, she turned to him and said, "Alex, I'd like you to meet Officer Mike Thompson."

Alex held out his hand and Mike shook it. For a moment both men took the others measure. Celeste watched the exchange and rolled her eyes. Men.

Finally Alex broke the silence. "It's nice to meet you Officer Thompson."

"Mike," Celeste interrupted. "Can you tell us anything about what happened here?"

The smile vanished from his face, his eyes hardened, and he shook his head. "It's such a shame. Some young girl was found this morning, throat slit. There's no blood so the detectives believe she was killed somewhere else and dumped here." He pointed over his shoulder to the alley were two men from the coroner's office were loading a body bag into their van. A few feet away a detective was crouched down by the dumpster studying the spot where the body had been.

"What was the girl's name?"

Mike sighed. "You know I can't tell you that. Not until her family has been notified."

Celeste nodded. She knew, but she thought that she could at least take a shot. "So you know who she is?"

Realizing she had him, he reluctantly said, "yes." Then, as if deciding that she would just find out anyway, he added, "we found a student ID on her."

"Which school?"

"Celeste…"

"Okay. Okay. Can you at least give me a description of the girl?"

Ever since she had gotten the call from Joe she had a sinking feeling in the pit of her stomach. The face of the girl who had contacted her kept popping into her head, unbidden, along with the faces of Julie and Beth. She prayed that she was wrong. She hoped that this was just a coincidence. Young girls went missing every day and, unfortunately, many ended up dead. There was no reason to believe that this girl had any connection to Dimitri and The Lair. Most likely she was just another unfortunate soul who ended up in the wrong place at the wrong time.

Mike seemed to hesitate, debating over how much to tell her. Seeing this, Celeste pleaded, "please. What could possibly be the harm?"

As she held her breath he seemed to give her words some thought, then relented. "Alright," he said on a sigh. "Early twenties. Long dark hair. A little on the thin side. She had a nose ring, but no other distinguishing marks such as tattoos or visible scars."

Celeste let out the breath she had been holding. She felt sick. He had just described the girl. Though she had tried to convince herself that it wasn't her, deep down Celeste had known it all along. "And which school did you say she was from again?"

"I didn't." He gave her an 'I'm not falling for any of your tricks' look.

"Right. Well, thank you for your time Mike." He nodded and stepped away.

Celeste walked back to the car, Alex following. "So what now?" He asked as they got in.

"We need to go to Tulane."

"The university? Why?" He seemed puzzled by her response and waited for her to answer his question.

"I have a hunch."

He started the car, but didn't pull out. Instead he turned in his seat and looked at her. "Mind letting me in on this hunch of yours?"

"I think that this girl is my contact. She was friends with Julie Simmons. They went to school together. Julie went to Tulane."

"So, that means that the girl went to Tulane. And Officer Thompson said they found a student ID on this girl," he said, following her train of thought.

"If this girl is my contact, which I believe she is, then we will most likely find answers at the university. She and Julie were friends. She was with Julie when Julie went missing, but was too scared to come forward. That's why she called me." Celeste flipped her laptop open and started tapping away at the keys. Without looking up at Alex she said, "I think that the key to finding out who this girl is, is to talk to Julie's roommate. She would know more than anyone who Julie's friends were."

Alex nodded and turned his attentions back to the road. As they headed for Tulane the car fell silent. Alex concentrated on traffic and Celeste continued to type away, oblivious to the chaos of a typical morning commute in the city.

CHAPTER 37

As the car finally rolled to a stop, Celeste looked out the window across a well-manicured lawn to the massive stone building beyond. Gibson Hall. One of the oldest structures on the Tulane campus, it stood as a sentry, greeting all who entered.

Glancing back at Alex she said, "keep going and make a right on Broadway. Julie's dorm is at the corner of Broadway and Plum. It's the Josephine Louise House. A big brick building. You can't miss it." Alex nodded. The car began to move forward and Celeste bent her head back down to study her computer. Within minutes the car came to a stop again.

"We're here," Alex said. Celeste looked up at the familiar building. She had been here once before to speak to Julie's roommate right after Julie had gone missing.

Slipping her laptop back in its bag she opened the door and stepped out onto the sidewalk. The blinding sun beat down on her and, though it was still morning, the temperature was rising quickly and the heat was already making itself known. Removing the light cardigan she had thrown on when they left the house, she tossed it into the backseat and slammed the car door shut.

By that time Alex had rounded the car and he came up beside her, placing a hand on the small of her back to guide her down the sidewalk. This simple gesture caused butterflies in her stomach and she caught her breath. It amazed her that a simple touch from this man could have such an effect on her. This also concerned her as things between them seemed to be moving very quickly, and she was still trying to process the fact that he wasn't exactly human. As if relationships weren't hard enough…..

She looked up at Alex to see if he had been equally affected, but his dark glassed hid his eyes and any emotions that she may have seen in them. His jaw was relaxed and his lips were set in a thin line. He appeared to be quite at ease and not affected by anything at that moment.

Celeste felt a bit disappointed, and slightly angry, at this fact. She was actually falling for the man, but he didn't seem to be as enamored.

Thankfully, they had arrived at the door and Celeste pushed those thoughts to the back of her mind. She turned her thoughts, instead, to the imminent meeting with Julie's roommate, mentally preparing herself by going over the questions she wanted to ask and the possible answers she might hear.

Alex ushered her through the door. As she had been there before, and knew the way to Julie's room, they bypassed the service desk and headed for the stairs.

The room was on the second floor at the end of a long hall. As it was midmorning on a week day most of the students were already in class and the hallway was empty. They made their way towards the far end of the corridor, the sound of Celeste's heels clicking along the floor echoing loudly off the walls. At the last door on the left she stopped and knocked, hoping that the room's occupant was still in. There was no response and no sound of movement within. She was just about to raise her hand and knock one more time when the door slowly opened, and a disheveled, sleepy-eyed young woman wearing pink pajama bottoms and a matching tank top appeared. It was apparent that Celeste had just awoken her and she didn't seem to be too thrilled about it.

Celeste smiled. "Hi, Stacy. I don't know if you remember me. My names Celeste Boucher. I spoke to you a few weeks ago about your missing roommate Julie. I'm sorry to disturb you, but I was wondering if we could have a moment of your time?"

The young woman's eyes narrowed on Celeste. "Yeah, I remember you. You're that reporter, right?"

"Yes, I am." The woman's eyes cut to Alex, roaming over him appreciatively. "This is Alex. An associate of mine," Celeste said through clenched teeth, not at all sorry now about disturbing the woman.

Alex flashed his charming smile. "It's nice to meet you Stacy. May we come in?"

All signs of sleepiness were completely erased from Stacy's eyes as she beamed up at Alex. Opening the door wider she stepped back. "Sure. Come on in."

As Celeste stepped into the room she noted the signs of a typical teenager's dorm room. Two beds-one neatly made and the other recently slept in- dominated the room. A small desk sat in the corner and a dresser stood against the far wall. Posters of the latest bands were hanging on the walls and clothes were scattered about the floor. It was obvious that Stacy's favorite color was pink as, along with her pajamas, the unmade bed was covered in pink sheets and pillows, and pink curtains hung in the one window.

Stepping over a pile of clothes Celeste sat down on the edge of the made-up bed, Alex sitting next to her. Stacy plopped herself cross legged in the center of her own bed and grabbed up a pillow to cradle in her lap. "I don't know what else I can tell you about Julie. You probably already know that they haven't found her yet."

Celeste looked at Alex. There was a warning in his eyes and she gave him a slight nod in acknowledgement. As much as she would like to tell Stacy the truth, she knew that it was best to just let her continue to believe that Julie was just missing. Looking back at Stacy, Celeste said, "Yes, I know. The thing is, I'm doing a follow up story and had a few more questions for you." At Stacy's nod Celeste asked, "did Julie have any close friends here?"

"Well...Julie liked to keep to herself. I convinced her to go out a couple of times with me and some of my friends, but she never seemed to enjoy herself. She really never got into the party scene and I finally just gave up asking her." Stacy tilted her head to the side in thought. "You know...now that I'm thinking about it, about two months ago Julie started hanging out with this girl. They shared a class together, but I don't remember which one. I know that they went out a few times, but they mostly hung out either here or at her dorm. She lives across campus."

"Do you remember the girl's name?"

"Brianna....Matthews. I think her last name was Matthews."

"Can you tell me what she looks like?"

"I don't have to." Stacy jumped off the bed and went to the desk. Opening a drawer she pulled a digital camera out and scanned through the photos on it. "This is Julie's camera. Her parents haven't come to get her stuff yet. I guess they still think she's coming back." She shrugged her shoulders indifferently. "Anyway, one day Julie asked me to take a pic of her and Brianna. It should still be on here. Here it is!" She handed the camera over to Celeste, and Celeste looked down at the picture of Julie and Brianna. It was her. Brianna was her contact.

Sighing, she handed the camera back to Stacy. "Thank you, Stacy." She rose and stepped towards the door. "And thank you for taking the time to answer my questions."

"No problem." Stacy's eyes went to Alex and she gave him a sultry smile. "Anytime."

Celeste rolled her eyes and opened the door, stepping out into the hallway. Alex followed her out, closing the door behind him.

"So?" he asked, raising a questioning brow.

"It was her."

Alex nodded solemnly. Taking her hand he gave it a squeeze and led her down the stairs and out of the building.

They went to Brianna's dorm next. Unfortunately, no one there seemed to know much about her, just that she seemed to keep to herself. Just like Julie. When they knocked on her door there was no answer and they soon gave up.

By the time they made it back to Alex's car, Celeste was feeling deflated. She thought that she would come here and get the answers she needed, and she did, but she still ended up leaving with more questions. Climbing in, she slammed the door and laid her head back on the headrest. "It doesn't seem right. Those poor girls go missing and end up dead, and no one seems to care."

Alex glanced over at her, but remained silent. Starting the car he put it in drive and pulled out into traffic.

CHAPTER 38

By the time they made it back to Alex's house Sam was already there, waiting for them on the front porch. As they climbed the steps he rose from the rocking chair he had been occupying and greeted them. "How did it go?" he asked.

Celeste ignored his questions and continued into the house. Raising a questioning brow to Alex, Alex shook his head. "Turns out the dead girl was the same girl from The Lair. She was friends with Julie Simmons."

Sam nodded his head in understanding and followed Alex into the house. Celeste was nowhere in sight as they went into the living room to talk. Sinking onto the sofa Alex asked, "What about you?"

"Nothing new."

***

Celeste pulled her laptop out and placed it on the bed. Sitting down next to it she opened it up and began typing away. She had written most of the brief while in the car, but she still had some finishing touches to add to it.

Her cell phone took that moment to ring and she slid it out of her pocket. "Hey, Joe."

"How did things go this morning?"

"Just as I expected. A young girl was found in an alley. Her throat was slit."

"I just got word that they released the girl's name."

"Brianna Matthews, right?"

There was a pause then Joe asked, "how did you know?"

"I had a hunch. I found out that she and Julie Simmons went to school together and were friends. I think that she knew what happened to Julie and died because of it."

"Interesting. What else did you find?"

"Not much. It seems she kept to herself, just like Julie. No one could really tell me much about her. I was able to dig up some information on the internet though. It seems that she was a transfer from up north-not a local-so it's going to be hard to contact her family."

"How's that brief coming?"

"I'm pretty much done, just need to add a few more

things. I'll email it to you in a few minutes."

"Good. I'll keep an eye out for it."

Celeste slipped the phone back into her pocket and read over what she had on the screen. She shook her head. It was just so sad. This poor girl's life was reduced to a few words that most people would scan over then never give a second thought to.

She thought about Brianna's family, so far away, receiving word over the phone that their daughter had been murdered. Left in some dirty alley. The pain must be unbearable.

Sighing, she hit the send button and snapped the computer shut. Leaving it on the bed she left the room and headed down the stairs.

She found Alex and Sam in the living room, deep in conversation. When she walked in they both stopped talking and looked up at her. She sat down next to Alex. "What's up?" she asked.

"Our boy here has the foolish idea of taking on Dimitri alone," Sam stated, then relaxed back into his chair, watching her reaction.

Celeste's eyes widened in shock, then narrowed as anger set in. Turning in her seat to look at him, she smacked Alex on the arm. "Are you crazy? You could get hurt."

***

Alex stood up and walked across the room. "I will be just fine. This is the only option."

"I could go with you," Sam said.

Alex looked at both of them. "No, Sam. I need you here with Celeste."

"Well, I'm not staying behind while you go out and get yourself killed." Celeste crossed her arms over her chest, that stubborn look in her eyes.

Alex sighed. He really didn't have the time to deal with this. "Look. I can't do this unless I know that you're safe, and I'll only feel that way if I know that you're here with Sam looking after you. If you come you will only be a distraction and both of us could be killed."

Celeste was fuming. "Then why can't Sam go and you stay here with me."

"Because this is my fight not Sam's," Alex snapped at her, his patience finally running out.

Celeste jumped to her feet and stormed over to him. Standing toe to toe she glared up at him unflinchingly. "And that is your problem. You are too emotionally involved in this and you're not thinking clearly. You're telling *me* that isn't dangerous?"

"You don't understand. You didn't sit by and watch, doing nothing, as he killed your best friend."

Her anger seemed to cool somewhat at his words and she said more calmly, "No, I didn't. I can't imagine how that feels, but I do know that this isn't right. Please stay and talk to Sam. Maybe together both of you can come up with a better plan."

"No."

Celeste threw her hands up in the air in frustration. "Fine. Go. Get yourself killed. I don't care." Spinning on her heel she stomped out of the room. A moment later Alex heard the bedroom door slam shut.

Alex looked over at Sam who was sitting back in his chair, watching the scene unfold before him with some amusement. If Sam had any doubts before about Celeste then he shouldn't now. She had fought Alex tooth and nail trying to convince him not to go through with this. Her feelings had been so evident, but Alex didn't want to think about it. He had to focus on Dimitri.

"Well, that went well," Sam said.

Alex glared at him. "She'll calm down and realize that I'm right."

Sam looked at Alex skeptically. "Really? You've been around long enough now that you should know that's not going to happen."

"Well, she is just going to have to deal with it because I'm not changing my mind. This is my only chance, I have to take it."

"I realize that you won't listen to reason with Celeste. Will you listen to me?" He glared at Sam, and Sam shrugged his shoulders. "I'm just saying that she has a point."

"Sam-"

Sam held up a hand to silence him, then leaned forward and braced his elbows on his knees. "Look. I understand how you feel, and if I were in your shoes I would be doing the same thing. But Dimitri is very powerful and he plays dirty. I know that you can hold your own in a fight, but maybe this one is too much for you to handle."

"Are you telling me that you're pulling me off this one? That you're going to bring someone else in to finish this?" Alex fisted his hands and bared his fangs as the anger rolled off of him.

Sam appeared to give this some thought. Alex knew that Sam had the power to call him off, and he would be forced to obey, but his friend also knew how he felt. Alex needed to finish this thing on his own. If he didn't then he would never be able to put all of this behind him, and Sam knew that.

Finally Sam shook his head. "No, I'm not bringing anyone else in. Though I think this is a bad idea, I won't try to stop you."

Alex relaxed, his fangs retracting. "Good." Turning to the window he looked out into the dark night and said, "I better get going," but he didn't move. Instead, he let his eyes wander up to the ceiling. "But there's something I should do first," he said quietly.

CHAPTER 39

Celeste was seething. There had been a cold, hard look in Alex's eyes, one that she had never seen before, and she knew that no matter what she said he wouldn't listen. She couldn't get that look out of her head.

Pacing back and forth she mumbled to herself, "why are men so pig headed?" Why couldn't Alex see how dangerous this was? He was too stubborn to admit that he might need help, and because of it he could get himself killed.

That thought caused her to catch her breath, pain stabbing through her chest. She couldn't lose him. Not now.

When she heard the door open she steeled herself and spun around, her anger returning. "Your still here?"

Alex heard the anger and contempt in her voice and he cringed inwardly. "I wanted to say goodbye." She turned her back to him, and the silence hung heavy between them.

She hadn't heard him move, which wasn't surprising, but felt him close behind her. Then she felt his hand brushing her hair aside. When she felt his lips on her neck she closed her eyes and bit her lip, trying to hold on to her anger. Anger was good. It kept her from feeling other things.

He wrapped his arms around her middle and pulled her back against him. "Why can't you understand?" he whispered in her ear.

Tears sprang to her eyes and she turned in his arms. Cupping his face in her hands she said, "why can't you see how dangerous and foolish this is?"

She knew that all the fear and pain that she was feeling shone through her tears, and she could see that he was affected by this. Without saying a word he lifted her up off her feet, so that they were eye to eye, and kissed her.

Her head was spinning. For a brief moment she forgot everything and opened herself up to him, taking him in and giving as much as she got. When he finally broke the kiss she took in a gulp of air, trying to steady her pulse.

***

Alex tried to convey all of the feelings that were ricocheting through him in that one kiss and it had left them both breathless.

Pressing his forehead to Celeste's, he closed his eyes. Trying to savor the moment. The pull to stay here wrapped in her arms was great, but he knew he had to leave. Reluctantly, he let her slide down the length of his body until her feet hit the floor, but he did not let her go. Looking deep into her eyes he said, "I'll be back soon. I promise." Celeste nodded, but didn't speak. He could tell that she was trying to fight back the tears.

Leaning forward he brushed his lips across her forehead and she closed her eyes. When she opened them he was gone.

CHAPTER 40

Celeste had made sure she composed herself before heading back downstairs. She walked into the living room, expecting to find Sam there, but it was empty. *Where could he be?* Going back out into the entrance she noticed the light on in the kitchen and decided that he must be in there. When she walk through the door she found him leaning against the counter, drinking a glass of blood as if it were the most natural thing in the world.

"Hello," he said, a lazy smile playing on his lips. He raised the glass to her in a salute then took a drink. He made no attempt to hide it like Alex had.

"Hi," she mumbled.

His brows rose questioningly. "Does this bother you?" He gestured to the glass.

"No, go ahead. I'm getting used to it." She opened the refrigerator and the corner of her mouth twitched into a halfhearted smile. Alex had completely stocked it with everything from milk and eggs to ketchup and *barbeque sauce?* She shook her head as she grabbed a yogurt and pulled the top off. Opening the drawer to her right she snatched up a spoon then plopped down at the kitchen table. Looking down at the white concoction she idly stirred the spoon around, realizing that her appetite had vanished.

Sam downed the last of the blood and rinsed the glass in the sink. Walking over he pulled out the chair opposite her and sat down. "Is that any good?"

"What?" She looked up at him, confused.

He pointed to the yogurt.

"Oh. Yes, it's good." She licked the very tip of the spoon. "Yum," she said with feigned enthusiasm.

"He knows what he's doing. He'll be alright," Sam said, reassuringly.

"I know."

"How about we watch television. I find it an amusing distraction."

"No, thank you. I'm not really in the mood."

"Alright. How about we play a game? I'm sure I could scrounge up a deck of cards."

"I know that you're trying to help, but I'm just not in the mood to do much of anything. In fact, I think I would just like to be alone for a while." Standing up she threw the uneaten cup of yogurt in the trash and tossed the spoon in the sink. "I'm just going to go upstairs."

Sam put his hands up in defeat and watched her walk out of the room. What she didn't see was him standing up and quietly slipping out the back door.

***

Celeste closed the bedroom door and tiptoed across the room, hoping that Sam wouldn't hear. *Why do they have to have such excellent hearing?* Reaching for the doorknob to the balcony she slowly turned it and opened the door, looking over her shoulder to make sure that Sam hadn't snuck up on her. As she slipped out she carefully closed the door behind her, making sure that she didn't make a sound.

"Going somewhere?"

Celeste jumped and let out a squeak. Her heart stopped then pounded wildly, nearly bursting in her chest. Spinning around she spied Sam in the shadows, leaning against the wall. His arms were crossed over his chest and a smile was fixed in place. He patiently waited for her to respond.

Celeste slapped a hand to her chest and tried to take a breath. "Are you trying to give me a heart attack?" As her heart began to slow she glared at him. "What are you doing out here?"

"I could ask you the same question."

She fidgeted under his watchful stare. "I…I just needed some air."

"Well, you've gotten some air, so let's get back inside." He pushed away from the wall and reached around her to open the door. With his hand on the knob he stopped, his smile disappearing completely.

The look on his face unsettled her and she whispered, "is something wrong?"

His eyes cut to hers and what she saw there sent a chill of fear running up her spine. "Stay here," he commanded.

He opened the door and Celeste caught a glimpse of three men dressed in black with ski masks covering their faces barreling through the bedroom door. Sam was on them instantly, grabbing the first one and tossing him across the room as if he weighed nothing. The other two men leapt on him, beating him with their fists. Their efforts were for naught, though, as Sam easily divested himself of them. Unfortunately, during the scuffle the first man had managed to push himself to his feet. Celeste watched in horror as he pulled a gun and pointed it at Sam.

"Sam! Look out!" She cried out to him just as the gun went off, but it was too late. Sam staggered back and fell to the floor, blood spreading across his chest. "No!" Celeste started forward, but was grabbed from behind and lifted off her feet. She screamed, kicking her legs fruitlessly and clawing at the arms encircling her. A hand clamped over her mouth.

A raspy voice close to her ear said, "it would be better for you if you cooperated."

Celeste recognized the voice. Roman. Dimitri's henchman. Her eyes widened and she stopped kicking. She knew that she could never fight him off.

"Good girl." His breath was hot against her flesh and she winced. Glancing at Sam she willed him to get up and fight, but he just laid there. Lifeless.

Hopelessness filled her and she closed her eyes. *Alex, where are you?*

CHAPTER 41

Alex sat in the dark, waiting. He usually thought of himself as a patient man, but not tonight. The urge to get up and pace about the room consumed him. Instead, he sat, watching the door and glancing at his watch every few minutes. He had expected Dimitri to have shown up by now. *Where is he?*

As he checked his watch for what seemed like the hundredth time, he allowed his thoughts to stray to Celeste. The woman was quite a mystery; caring and gentle one minute, strong willed and frustratingly stubborn the next. He had never known anyone like her, and that was saying something.

He never thought that he would ever love another woman again. He had been so careful for so long, but she had somehow wormed her way into his heart before he even realized what was happening. *But how can we possibly make it work?*

That was the problem. He was a vampire, something that had cost him the one other woman he had ever loved.

He realized that things had changed drastically since then, but it was still a major obstacle. One that he wasn't sure that Celeste would be willing or able to take on, and he wasn't sure if he wanted to put her through that.

A faint sound outside the door drew his attention and he bolted from his chair. He was across the room in an instant, looking through the peephole. Dimitri stood on the other side, one fist rising to knock. Alex opened the door before he had the chance, though, and grabbed Dimitri, slamming him up against the wall.

Dimitri didn't fight him, instead he said in a calm voice, "now, now Alexandru. You really need to work on your anger. It seems like it's becoming an issue."

Alex released him, but reached for the sword he had placed in the corner. Taking it up, he placed the blade against Dimitri's neck. "Now you will get what you deserve."

"I wouldn't do that if I were you," Dimitri warned.

"Why not? I have the upper hand now, Dimitri. There's nothing stopping me."

"Are you sure about that?" His eyes narrowed on Dimitri and Dimitri laughed. "Do you know where your little human is, Alexandru?"

"Celeste?" Dimitri smiled. "What have you done with her," Alex shouted.

"Me?" Dimitri feigned innocence. "I didn't do anything with her." His evil smile grew. "But my associates will not be so kind to her if I'm not back within the hour."

Rage shot through Alex, but he lowered the sword.

How did Dimitri get to Celeste, and where was Sam? Can I even believe that Dimitri has her? Dimitri wasn't exactly a trustworthy person. It was possible that he was just bluffing, but Alex just couldn't take that chance. "What do you want?"

"What do I want?" Dimitri tapped a finger against his lips as if in thought. "Well….what I would really like is to run my business without being accosted every time I turn around." Dimitri strolled over and sat in the chair that Alex had vacated only moments before. Leaning back he crossed his legs and looked at Alex. "That is why I came here actually. I have a proposition for you." He gestured towards the sofa. "Please, sit."

Alex didn't move. "Get on with it Dimitri."

Dimitri sighed, "Fine. It's simple enough really, you leave me alone, for good, and I give you back the girl." When Alex opened his mouth to respond Dimitri cut him off. "I'll give you some time to think about it. You can come by The Lair later tonight with your answer." He rose and walked up to Alex. "Ms. Boucher and I will be waiting." He strolled out the door leaving Alex completely alone.

CHAPTER 42

"Celeste! Sam!" Alex called out their names, looking around the house frantically. He had rushed home to find the door had been busted open and the house completely still. There was no sign of a struggle anywhere on the first floor and he raced to the stairs.

With his foot on the first step he stopped. Sam appeared at the top of the staircase looking weak and defeated. Blood soaked his shirt.

Alex rushed to his side. Putting a shoulder under Sam's arm he helped him down the stairs and into the living room, depositing him on the sofa. "What the hell happened here?"

Sam shook his head. "There were three of them, Alex. Humans. It was an easy enough fight, but one of the bastards pulled a gun and got off a shot before I could get to him." He waved a hand at his chest. "When I came to they were gone, and so was Celeste. I'm sorry."

"Damn it." Alex began pacing back and forth, thrusting his fingers through his hair. *He really does have her.*

The knot in his stomach tightened. There was no telling what Dimitri would do to her. Fear like he had never known overwhelmed him and he growled, punching a hole in the wall. "I have to get her back." Without another thought he headed across the room towards the door.

"Wait." Sam's hand shot out and gripped Alex by the arm. Though he appeared weak after his ordeal he still possessed enough strength to stop Alex in his tracks. "You have to think about this. You can't just go charging in there in this state. Celeste could get hurt."

He shook off Sam's grip, but he didn't leave. Instead he dropped down onto the sofa next to Sam, and buried his face in his hands. "Your right. I need a plan."

"We need a plan." Alex lifted his head and looked at Sam. "You don't think I'm just going to sit here while you have all the fun do you."

"Sam-"

"I'll be fine. The wound has already begun to heal. All I need now is to regain my strength. Just get me some blood and I'll be as good as new by the time we figure this plan out."

Alex looked at him skeptically, but didn't argue. "Fine. I'll be right back." He stood up and headed for the kitchen, returning shortly with a bottle.

Sam took the bottle and looked up at him. "You couldn't nuke it in the microwave first?" He glared at Sam and Sam shook his head. "I know, I know. Now is not the time for jokes." Alex watched as Sam tipped his head back and downed half the bottle. Though the blood was cold Alex knew that it would slake Sam's thirst, and he knew that Sam should already feel his strength returning.

Alex resumed pacing in front of the fireplace. "I need to think," he said in frustration, unable to concentrate. A dozen thoughts raced through his head. He pictured all of the worst possible things that Dimitri could be doing to Celeste, and the anger rolled over him in waves. He was so consumed with rage he couldn't seem to think straight. He had to calm down.

He was so preoccupied with his thoughts that he had all but forgotten about Sam until Sam cleared his throat and spoke up. "I may have an idea." Alex stopped and looked at him. "Dimitri expects you to just walk right in there with your answer." Alex continued to stare at him. "Well, let's give him what he wants. You."

"If I walk in there and give Dimitri my word that I will not interfere again he will never accept it. I'll just end up handing myself over to him, then how in the hell do I get Celeste out of there? He is not a man of his word. He won't just let her go once he has me."

"No, he won't. But if you walk in there with a clear head, and me by your side, then you might stand a chance of getting Celeste out of there unharmed." Sam thought a moment. "You know, there is a lot of animosity between the two of you. Maybe if you provoke him enough to distract him, which I am sure will be easy for you to do, then I might be able to sneak Celeste out." When he looked at Sam skeptically Sam said, "Your right. That won't work."

Silence filled the room again as both men lost themselves in thought. Finally Sam said, "what about a back door. You've been in there. You know the layout, right?"

Alex shook his head. "There is no way to sneak in without being noticed. The only entrance into his private apartments is through the club. There is a long corridor, lined with doors, that splits at the end. To the right are Dimitri's private rooms and to the left is an exit door. As far as I know there are no other entrances or exits, and there is no telling which room he will have her in."

Sam gave this some thought and let out an exaggerated sigh. "Well, I'm all out of ideas. I guess we will just have to do it your way."

Looking at Sam with a raised brow, he asked, "and what way is that?"

"The usual way. We both go charging in there together. Guns blazing, so to speak." Sam pushed to his feet.

"That isn't funny."

"No it's not." Sam looked over at Alex. "Ready?"

CHAPTER 43

"Let me go you son of a bitch!" Celeste pulled her arm, struggling against Roman's steely grip and knowing it was useless. Roman ignored her, dragging her along behind him until they came to the same door were she had first encountered Alex. The image of that moment flashed through her head and she wondered if he was alright, if she would ever see him again. Before she could dwell on it though, Roman pushed her through the door and into the middle of a large, well-furnished room.

An oversized armchair sat directly in front of her, its high back blocking her view of the occupant. As she stood there staring, an arm raised from the armrest and motioned her closer. When she remained rooted to the spot Roman propelled her forward until she was standing in front of the chair, and the man in it.

"Hello, my dear. I'm so glad that we finally get to meet. Officially." Dimitri smiled up at her. His eyes roamed over her, and she was glad that she hadn't eaten that yogurt earlier because she had a feeling she wouldn't have been able to keep it down at that moment. He waved a hand at the chair opposite him. "Please, sit. Relax. We have a lot to discuss."

"I don't have anything to say to you." Though the urge to defy him was great she prudently took a seat. She quickly scanned the room as she did so, looking for any possible way of escape. Her heart sank when she realized that the only way in or out was through the door she had come through, and Dimitri was between her and it. Even if she did manage to get past him, which was unlikely to say the least, she still had to contend with his muscle, Roman, who stood sentry by the door. *I'm so screwed.*

"Well, that may be, but I have something to say to you." Dimitri leaned forward and stared hard at Celeste. The dark depths of his eyes held no life. They were nothing but black, empty orbs. Celeste held back the shudder that ran through her body and held his stare, head high. She refused to show this man any fear.

Dimitri seemed to find this curious. Tilting his head to the side he seemed to contemplate her reaction to him. "You are very brave my dear, but bravery can be foolish." Abruptly he leaned back in his chair. Resting his elbows on the armrests he entwined his fingers and pursed his lips in thought. "You believe that your precious Alexandru will come to your rescue, but I'm afraid that you are mistaken."

Fear and apprehension flashed momentarily in her eyes, but she quickly blinked them away. In a calm tone, which was surprising even to her own ears, she asked, "what have you done with Alex?"

He appeared taken aback by her words, as if he could never harm someone. "Why, nothing at all. He is perfectly fine. In fact, I expect him any moment."

Involuntarily, Celeste's eyes darted to the door. It remained closed.

Seeing her reaction Dimitri chuckled. "Patience my dear, you will see him soon enough. In the meantime, though, I do have one question for you. Exactly how well do you know your lover?"

Celeste's eyes narrowed on him, but she didn't answer. What was he getting at? What did he seem to know that he thought she didn't? It was true that she and Alex had only known each other for a very short time, but she had thought that he had been up front with her. Well, mostly. After all, he had told her he was a vampire. That's a pretty big secret to trust someone with.

Granted, she also knew that she couldn't possibly know everything about him. There were probably plenty of things that she didn't know that only a person who had been with someone long enough would pick up. Habits, likes, dislikes, idiosyncrasies, those sort of things. However, she didn't believe that those were what Dimitri was referring to.

"Has he told you about his past?" Dimitri inquired.

"Of course."

"Ah, then he must have told you what a coward he is."

Celeste fumed. "He is no coward. *You* are the coward."

"Really? If memory serves me right, it was Alex who stood idly by and watched as his best friend, and maker, died. He was too afraid to stop it. That sounds like a coward to me. What do you think?" When Celeste refused to answer he said, "when his back is against the wall, Alexandru has a tendency to turn tail and run. If I were you I would not depend on him to save you."

CHAPTER 44

"Wait." Sam put a hand on Alex's arm as he reached for the door to enter The Lair. "Maybe it would be better if we go in separately. You should go in first and I'll follow in a minute."

Alex nodded his head and opened the door. When he stepped inside the first thing he noticed was that the noise level was lower than it had been on his previous trips. The crowd seemed to be cut in half too. It was probably because there was no band on the stage tonight.

Scanning the bar he noted that the patrons were more subdued. They casually sat, sipping their drinks. Music was being pumped through the sound system, but it was not as loud as the band was and there were only a handful of people on the dance floor.

Skirting the dancers he edged along the wall until he made it to the stage. Pulling the curtain back he spied Sam walking into the club. Their eyes met and an unspoken message passed between them. Sam nodded and headed for the bar. Alex slipped behind the curtain.

Making his way down the hall, he stopped outside of the room where he had first kissed Celeste. Placing a hand on the doorknob he paused, took a deep breath, and opened the door.

Celeste was sitting in front of him. Her eyes flew up to meet his and he could see concern and fear emanating from them. The anger that he thought he had under control threatened to take over, and he had to will himself to calm down and assess the situation.

Roman stood beside the door, only a few feet away. Though he had not moved when Alex walked in he was definitely ready for a fight. No other goons appeared to be in the room, so Alex focused his attention on the chair opposite Celeste's.

Dimitri's voice came from the chair. "Alexandru, it is so nice of you to join us." In an instant Dimitri was out of his chair and behind Celeste, pulling her to her feet and holding her before him like a shield. "We were just having an interesting conversation about you."

Alex was losing the battle for control over his rage. He could see the silent pleading in Celeste's eyes. She wanted him to calm down and think before he reacted, but he ignored her and advanced towards them instead.

Before he made it a few steps Roman was on him, effortlessly flinging him across the room. He looked up and caught a glimpse of the sheer horror on Celeste's face right before Roman pounced on him. As Roman landed blow after blow Alex tried to fight back. He struggled to get the upper hand, but Roman was more powerful then he looked and it took all of Alex's efforts to fight off the blows, landing a few of his own.

Celeste was screaming now with everything she had

and within seconds Sam came crashing through the door. Alex could just imagine the look on Celeste's face at the sight of Sam. After all, the last time she had seen Sam he was lying in a pool of blood on the bedroom floor. She knew that vampires healed quickly, but he'd bet that she never imagined that Sam could have recovered that quickly after suffering such a devastating wound.

Sam pried Roman off of Alex and threw him to the floor. As the three of them were locked in combat Alex didn't see Dimitri dragging Celeste out of the room, and only became aware of the fact that Dimitri was racing down the hall and out into the alley because Celeste was screaming out his name.

If he had a heart he knew that it would have stopped beating at that moment. Fear washed over him like a bucket of ice cold water and he struggled to his feet.

"Go!" Sam shouted and he didn't hesitate. He raced after Dimitri and Celeste, bursting through the exit into the alley.

At the sound, Dimitri stopped and turned to face Alex as he flew at him. Dimitri flung Celeste aside just as Alex launched himself and they both fell to the ground.

***

As Alex and Dimitri rolled around on the dirty, damp, asphalt Alex managed to call out to Celeste, "Run!"

but she stood, frozen in place.

She knew that she should listen to Alex and run as fast and as far as she could, but her legs refused to move. She had to stay. There was no way she could leave Alex, though there was nothing she could do to help him. Or was there...

She looked around the dimly lit alley, squinting through the darkness, searching for anything that could be used as a weapon. Spotting the dumpster to her right she ran to it, ready to rummage through it for anything that could help Alex, but she was grabbed from behind. Caught off guard she struggled, kicking and cursing.

"Calm down." Sam's deep voice rang in her ears and she instantly stilled, looking up at him pleadingly.

"I have to help him."

"No." That one word was spoken with such forcefulness that Celeste blinked up at him in surprise. "He has to do this on his own."

"But-"

"No." Sam's arm tightened around her and she looked on helplessly.

***

Dimitri landed an unexpected blow to Alex's jaw and

Alex rolled to the side, stunned. Seeing the advantage Dimitri took it, jumping on him and pinning him to the ground.

Dimitri's hands wrapped around Alex's neck and Alex clawed at them, trying to pry them loose. But he knew that his efforts were fruitless. Dimitri was much older than Alex and, therefore, was much more powerful.

Alex looked up at Dimitri and saw the crazed, murderous eyes of a madman. He knew that Dimitri wouldn't stop until he was dead, and then he would go right after Celeste. Alex had to stop him, once and for all, so he released his hold on Dimitri's wrists and flung his arm out, feeling for anything that he could use as a weapon. Out of the corner of his eye he spied a pile of broken pallets piled haphazardly against the wall and he reached towards them. Stretching his fingers as far as they would reach, the tips bumped against something cold and hard, and he worked it closer. Wrapping his hand around the thick, broken piece of wood he brought it up and thrust it deep into Dimitri's chest.

Shock washed over Dimitri's face as he realized what had happened. Falling to the side he grabbed at the makeshift stake and pulled it out. It fell from his fingers to the ground, the sound of it hitting the asphalt echoing in the silent alley.

Before their eyes Dimitri disintegrated into a pile of ash. At the sound of Celeste's gasp Alex's head snapped around and his eyes locked with hers. Celeste's hand flew up to cover her mouth, and the realization that it could have been him swept across her face. She began to struggle against Sam.

This time Sam let her go and she ran to him, dropping to her knees and throwing her arms around him, heedless of the fact that he was covered in blood and dirt. "Oh god!" She repeated the words over and over. Then, pulling back she scanned his face, taking in his bruised and battered appearance. "You poor thing. Look at you," she crooned, drawing his head against her chest.

Alex smiled at her reaction. He wasn't used to being coddled, and it was quite amusing. "I'm fine. It's over now." Gently disentangling himself from her, he pushed to his feet then reached down and helped her to hers.

Sam was by their sides by the time they were up. "Nice work," Sam said, slapping him on the back. "Don't worry, I'll report everything to the council. Roman has been detained and seems willing to talk, so there shouldn't be any problems."

Alex nodded his head. "Thanks." Putting his arm around Celeste he said, "Why don't we get out of here?"

CHAPTER 45

They drove back to Alex's house in silence. This was fine with Celeste as it gave her time to mull over the events of the night. *What do I do now?* She loved Alex, but could she live a life like this? Granted, there had been plenty of mystery and excitement-things that she lived for-but there had been plenty of danger too. *I could have been killed!*

Another thought crossed her mind, *Alex could have been killed.* She felt the pain in her chest as greatly has if it had happened. He had a dangerous job, one that would only cause her worry every moment of every day. Could she live with that?

She realized that Alex wasn't like other men. She knew that he could definitely take care of himself in a fight, but what if he went up against another vampire like he had just done. Dimitri was powerful, but she knew that there were others that were even more powerful. Next time he might not be as lucky. When she had watched, helplessly, as Alex fought off Dimitri, the fear that had consumed her was so great she didn't think that she could stand to go through that again.

The events of the night, coupled with the turmoil she was feeling within, made her tired and sick to her stomach. All she wanted right now was a nice comfortable bed to fall into, and to sleep for the next week. Damn the paper and her deadline. Chances were good that she wouldn't get fired anyway, as Joe would never be able to bring himself to do it. She would make up some excuse and he would accept it without question. Also, a good night's sleep would help her clear her mind and figure out what she would do about her and Alex.

As the car came to a stop she waited for Alex to open her door. She had come to realize that he enjoyed doing these little gentlemanly things for her, and she got a little thrill at them herself. Nowadays men just didn't seem to want to be bothered.

As she got out of the car she looked up into his face. He looked as bad as she felt, if not worse. Though the wounds had already healed during the ride, he was still dirty and bloody, his clothes were disheveled and ripped in places, and he looked even paler than usual. Unable to resist, she brushed a stray lock of hair from his forehead with her fingertips then trailed them down to his cheek, allowing them to linger there.

Smiling, Alex turned his head slightly to kiss her palm. Reaching up he took her hand and led her to the house. "Let's get you to bed. You look like you could use some rest," he said over his shoulder.

"Hey! You're one to talk."

He ignored her and led them into the house. Not stopping, he pulled her up the stairs and to the bedroom, leaving Sam to his own devices. As they hurried down the hall, Celeste looked back to find Sam heading for his own room. *I guess we all need some rest.*

Once in the bedroom Celeste planted herself on the edge of the bed. Alex went into the bathroom and a second later she heard the shower running. Popping his head out the door he motioned for her to join him.

"I'm too tired to move," she said with a slight pout.

"Then you don't have to." Walking over to her he bent and picked her up, cradling her in his arms. Though she was too exhausted to do much she did snuggle closer, laying her head on his strong shoulder. It felt so good she sighed in contentment.

Once in the bathroom he placed her on her feet and divested her of her clothes in record time. A moment later they were both naked and standing under the steaming spray of water. When she grabbed the shampoo bottle he took it from her hands. "Allow me," he said as he squeezed a generous amount into his palm. Snapping the cap shut he placed the bottle back on its ledge and began messaging the shampoo into her hair.

The rhythmic motion of his hands was so soothing that she closed her eyes and leaned into him. A smile crossed her lips and she moaned softly.

***

Alex watched as Celeste relaxed in pure pleasure, and he felt his own body respond. "Lean your head back," he said softly, and then rinsed the lather from her hair when she did so. Reaching for the soap he began to run it slowly over her body.

When he was done Celeste took the soap from his hands, a playful smile in place. "My turn," she said, eyeing him like a cat would a mouse.

Alex groaned. He wasn't sure he could take it, but he steeled himself as she ran her fingers across his chest and down his stomach. What was it about this woman that made him react so? After the night he had the last thing that he should be thinking of doing was taking Celeste against the shower wall. He was tired and weak from his run in with Dimitri, but suddenly it was as if he had found his second wind.

Unfortunately, he could see the toll that the night had taken on Celeste and he knew that it wouldn't be fair to her. She needed to rest, so he turned off the shower, grabbed a clean towel, and wrapped it around her. Then, drying himself off quickly, he picked her up and carried her to the bed, gently depositing her on the clean sheets and pulling the covers up to her chin. Climbing in beside her he pulled her close and held her as they both drifted off into sweet slumber.

CHAPTER 46

Celeste awoke slowly. She was first aware of strong arms wrapped tightly around her and she snuggled closer, savoring the feeling. Then, reluctantly, she opened her eyes.

A faint shaft of light shone through the curtains, so she knew that she had not slept the day away. Glancing at the clock she read the time, half past three. Sighing she turned slightly to look back at Alex. His face was relaxed in sleep and she marveled at how handsome he was. *What am I going to do?*

At that moment her stomach decided to let her know that she hadn't eaten in forever. Deciding that she could think and eat at the same time she disengaged herself from Alex's arms, carefully so as not to wake him, and slipped into the robe that had been carelessly tossed onto the end of the bed.

She tiptoed down the stairs and into the kitchen. Going right for the fridge she took out the milk and searched the cabinets. Just as she thought, Alex had stocked up on practically everything including cereal. She smiled, *he must have cleaned the store out*. Popping the top on the box she poured the cereal and milk into a bowl and carried it to the table.

As she shoveled spoonful after spoonful into her mouth she let her mind wander then settle on Alex. All of the doubts and trepidations from the night before cluttered her brain once more. The question was, now that Alex was in her life could she live without him?

Staring out the window she watched as a slight breeze rustled through the trees. The garden was in full bloom and the beauty of it took her breath away. As she stared in awe a thought hit her. Even after what had happed last night she realized that she had never felt more safe, and at peace, as when she was here with Alex. Suddenly, the thought of leaving him seemed more painful than the thought of living with the fear and worry of what he was. What he did.

She knew what she had to do.

***

Celeste studied herself in the mirror. The black lace of the teddy hugged her curves and accentuated the swells of her breasts. Smiling she ran her hands down her sides and turned from right to left. Satisfied with her appearance she looked over at Alex, still peacefully asleep. *Not for long* she thought with a mischievous grin.

Climbing onto the bed she crawled across it on her hands and knees until she was hovering over him. Leaning down she brushed her lips across his and trailed a finger along the hard muscles of his chest. Alex moaned and his eyelids fluttered then opened. Looking up he drank in the sight of her. Her hair was loose and falling in a mass of chestnut waves around her face, and the teddy clung to her body like a second skin, leaving nothing to the imagination.

Now fully awake, Alex snaked a hand around the back of her neck. Pulling her down, he kissed her hard, leaving her breathless.

Pulling back she stared down at him, a smile like warm honey spreading across her face. When he reached for her once more she brushed his hand away and shook her head. Then, straddling his hips, she leaned forward and pressed soft kisses across his chest, trailing her hands down his body as she did so. When she wrapped her fingers around his hard cock he sucked in a breath and thrust his fingers into her thick mass of dark hair, pressing her lips more firmly against his flesh.

Liquid fire slowly spread through her body. As the excitement grew her kisses became more urgent. She could feel the tenseness in his body and knew that he was ready for her. She knew that he was trying to hold back, waiting for her to make the next move, and the knowledge excited her even more.

Pulling back she looked down at him. Their eyes locked and held as she guided him inside her. Then, with one hard thrust, he was buried deep. She moaned and closed her eyes. Bracing her hands against his chest she began to move against him, slowly at first then with more urgency.

Gripping her hips, Alex met her thrust for thrust. As the pleasure took her over she threw her head back, crying out as she did so. Unable to hold back himself, Alex followed her over the edge.

Celeste collapsed onto Alex's chest, unable to move. She was aware of his hand coming up and brushing over her hair in a soothing gesture, and she nuzzled his neck. Content, she drifted off.

CHAPTER 47

Alex was aware the moment Celeste fell asleep. Her body relaxed and her breathing was even and deep. Not wanting to disturb her he remained still, idly rubbing a hand up and down her back.

It had been centuries since he had felt this way about a woman, but that little niggling of worry had persisted and now he couldn't ignore it. Last night had proven that this wouldn't work. Celeste had been put in harm's way and it was all his fault. If anything had happened to her....

He shook his head. No. He needed to end things now. He couldn't risk something like this happening again. He had already lost one woman he had loved and he was not going to lose another.

The only problem is, how can I bring myself to do it? He just didn't know if he had the strength.

As the thought crossed his mind he felt her stir against him, and she lifted her head. With her hair disheveled and her lips still swollen from his kisses she looked irresistible. When she smiled at him he was completely lost. She leaned down and pressed her lips against his.

For a brief moment Alex gave in, savoring what could be his last taste of her. After a lingering moment he broke the kiss and slid out from beneath her. It was best if he got this over with now, and he knew he would never be able to do it with her this close. Crossing the room he opened a drawer and pulled out a pair of sweats and a t-shirt. If he was going to do this it would definitely go better with clothes on.

***

Celeste watched as Alex dressed. His movements were stiff and his back was tense. Something had changed and she couldn't figure out why. Whatever it was, though, was not good and unease had her reaching for her robe. She wrapped it around herself like a protective shield.

Alex was still standing with his back to her and she waited, holding her breath. When he finally turned, the look in his eyes chilled her to the bone. Dread washed over her and she wondered what could have happened in the last few moments that would have caused him to do such a one-eighty.

"We need to talk."

She let the breath she was holding out on a long sigh, "Oh, great. Nothing good ever started with those words."

At any other time Alex would have smiled at her words, but not now. Sighing himself, he decided it would be best to just get to the point. *Why dance around the issue?* "I think that it would be best if we went our separate ways."

Celeste stared at him blankly. She heard the words, but she couldn't seem to process them. "What does that mean?" she thought out loud.

Thinking the question was directed at him, Alex responded, "I think it would be best for both of us if we broke things off now before things get too serious."

The words finally penetrated and Celeste narrowed her eyes. Anger began to boil in her veins and she jumped to her feet. "Before things get too serious?" She waved a hand at the bed. "This isn't serious?"

"I just meant-"

"How *dare* you?" she fired at him, cutting off his words. "You string me along and now when things do get serious you're ready to run for the door."

"It's not like that."

"Oh, give me a break." She began to pace back and forth, mumbling to herself. Occasionally she waved a hand in the air.

Alex seemed to watch her in stunned silence. She knew that she was babbling like a mad woman, and Alex looked as though he was afraid to speak for fear that she would attack. Unfortunately, staying quiet didn't save him because she suddenly whirled on him, her eyes shooting sparks.

"I know what this is really about." She pointed a

finger at him. "You are afraid."

"What?"

She ignored him, intent on continuing with her rant. "It's because of her isn't it?"

A coldness seemed to settle over him. When he spoke his words came out low and lethal. "You don't know what you're talking about."

She was aware of the dangerous territory that she was walking into, but she didn't care. He had hurt her too much and she wanted him to hurt as well. So, in anger, she lashed out at him. "Don't play dumb, Alex. I know about her."

"My past has nothing to do with this."

She knew that his control was beginning to slip and there was a distinct hardness in his voice. She pushed anyway. "Are you kidding me? Your past has everything to do with this. Whatever happened with this other woman has turned you into a coward who runs every time you get close to another woman."

She never saw him move, he was that quick. He was on her in an instant, grabbing her by the arms and shaking her so hard her head snapped back. She had never thought he would hurt her, but for the first time she doubted that. She experienced a slight tingling of fear and instinctively began to struggle.

Alex ignored her struggles, and she saw the control that he was always so careful to hold on to fall away. "That is a lie."

Hearing the underlying doubt and uncertainty in his voice, Celeste stopped struggling and looked deep into his eyes. "Is it?" she asked softly.

***

Alex pushed her away and turned his back to her, jamming his fingers through his hair in frustration. He wasn't angry at her words so much as the fact that she was right. But he couldn't tell her that. He still had his pride. But what did that get him, really?

Without Celeste life would be dull. He would be nothing but alone and miserable. He had lived that life for way too long and he found that it was getting old. The thought of a home and family with Celeste warmed him like nothing else ever had. Then realization washed over him like a bucket of ice cold water. How could he give Celeste a family? Vampires couldn't have children.

The fight seemed to go out of him and, almost in defeat he said, "I can't give you a normal life."

Celeste placed a hand on his arm and urged him to turn and look at her. When he did she said, "I don't want a normal life." She gave him a lopsided grin. "That would be boring, and I enjoy a little excitement."

"You don't understand." It was the second time he had said that and he could tell that it was starting to frustrate her. By the look in her eyes she really wanted to understand, and in order to do that he had to tell her the whole story. But he hesitated.

She had been right. Though she didn't know much about his past, she had hit the nail on the head when she accused him of being afraid. What had happened in the past had affected him deeply and to the point that he was afraid to commit to her.

"Tell me about her." He watched her steel herself as she said those words. She probably expected him to become furious and lash out at her as he had done before, but instead he sank down onto the bed and hung his head. Sitting next to him she rubbed a hand against his back in encouragement and support.

His first reaction was to close up, shut her out and distance himself. What had happened in his past had been too painful. He had never talked about Ana to anyone, save Sam, and it was hard to find the words, but he knew that if he told Celeste she would better understand his reasoning. Maybe then she could accept his decision.

Taking a deep breath he began, "Her name was Ana. We had known each other since we were children, and had loved each other just as long. We vowed that we would marry one day, when we were old enough. But then Stefan turned me and we ended up moving to another village. Ana and I didn't let that stop us from seeing each other though. Thankfully our villages were close enough that we could still steal away and meet often." He smiled wistfully at the memory, but then it quickly vanished. "I was still convinced that Ana and I still had a chance. Stefan had warned me that it was foolish, but I didn't listen. I didn't think of the consequences. I believed that we could get through anything because we were in love."

He rubbed a hand over his face as the memories flooded back, the pain robbing him of his next words. As if sensing this Celeste silently entwined her fingers with his and squeezed. That little encouragement was enough and he continued, "We married and things were good. I kept telling myself that I would explain things to her when the time was right, but it never was. Then one day I was in the forest feeding on a deer that I had just caught, and I heard a noise and looked up. Ana was coming through the trees. When she saw what was before her she froze in fear. I went to her to try and explain, but she turned and ran in a panic. When I caught her she fought with all her might. I had never seen such fear in a person before and that fear was of me. I immediately let her go, pain tearing at my heart, and she stumbled back away from me. She tripped. Before I could reach her she fell, striking her head. Ana died because of her fear for me."

***

Celeste could only imagine what he must have felt and her heart ached for him. "I'm so sorry." He raised his head and looked at her. The pain that she saw in his eyes brought tears to her own and she wrapped her arms around him in comfort. "I can't imagine what that must have been like for you, but you have to realize that I'm not her. When I learned what you were I didn't run away." She cupped his face in her hands. "I'm still here, Alex."

"I know." He shook his head and pulled away from her. "But I can't give you the life that you deserve. Just like I couldn't give Ana the life that she deserved."

Why are men so stubborn? Her short temper made itself known and she snapped at him. "Damn it Alex, why can't you see that I love you and that I accept you for who and what you are?" She watched as his eyes widened in surprise at her words, and she felt that same shock. She had never taken those words lightly, and had never said them to any man. She had realized and accepted her feelings for him, but she had not intended for those words to slip out like that, especially now.

"You love me?"

She wasn't going to back out now, so she stiffened her back and said with conviction, "yes."

He seemed to mull that over. "I love you too, but sometimes that just isn't enough."

He said this so matter-of-factly that Celeste almost missed it. "You love me too?" She said in astonishment.

"Of *course* I do. I just said it didn't I?" He got to his feet and began to move about the room like a caged lion. "But as I said, it's not enough."

Celeste watched him with some amusement. The fact that Alex actually loved her made her giddy. She wanted to jump up and throw herself into his arms, but she knew that that wasn't the best tactic. She had to tread lightly if she was going to make him come to his senses. She thought a moment, searching for just the right words. "Then, in your mind, what is enough?"

CHAPTER 48

He stopped and looked at her. She had caught him off guard with her casual question and he had to give it some thought. "For one, I can't give you a family. Children."

She nodded her head. "Okay. Well, I never did give children much thought. I was always focused on my career and was content with just that."

He looked at her as if he was seeing a completely different person. He expected most women to have a problem with that, but as he found time and time again, Celeste wasn't like most women. *She's full of surprises.* "What about the fact that I don't age and you do? How do you feel about that?"

"How do you feel about it?" She countered.

He hadn't really thought much about it, but when he answered it was truthfully, "I suppose I can accept it."

"Well, so can I."

She seemed to have a rational explanation for

everything and it was really starting to annoy him. He tried to think of something else, but nothing came to mind. He began to realize that maybe she was right. Maybe he was a coward who was just looking for excuses to hide the fact that he loved her so much and was afraid of losing her, which made his plans of pushing her away seem even more absurd.

Celeste must have seen the doubt in his eyes, and finally felt like she was winning the battle, because she rose and came to him. As if in an effort to tip the scales more in her favor she wrapped her arms around his neck and pressed against him. "Is that all you've got?" The words came out on a purr.

"Hmm?" With her body so close and her sweet scent filling his senses, Alex had a hard time concentrating on what she was saying.

"I said," she trailed a finger along his jaw and smiled when a muscle in his cheek ticked. "Is that all, or are there any other reasons why you think we won't work?"

"No," he mumbled, not really thinking about what he was saying. The need to kiss her was overwhelming. "That was it."

Her smile broadened and she rose up on her tiptoes to claim his lips with her own. "Then I guess that this conversation is over," she whispered against his skin.

In response, he picked her up and tossed her onto the bed, eliciting a squeal of surprise and delight from her, and climbed onto the bed himself.

EPILOGUE

Alex awoke to find the bed next to him empty. Looking around he found no sign of Celeste, so he slipped out of bed and threw on a pair of pants. Heading downstairs he found her in the kitchen, sitting at the table with a cup of coffee and her laptop. When he walked in she looked up and flashed him a brilliant smile. "Good morning sleepyhead. Or should I say good evening?"

Alex took a bottle of blood from the refrigerator, poured it into a mug, and placed it in the microwave. Walking over to Celeste he bent down and kissed the top of her head. "What are you doing?"

"Oh, I'm just finishing up my article."

The microwave beeped and he walked back over to it. "I thought you already sent your article in?" he called over his shoulder.

"No, that was just a brief for Brianna's death. This is a more in-depth article about all three girls, and the dangers of vampire cults in this city. People need to be aware."

Alex pulled one of the chairs closer to hers and took a seat. "Do you mind?" he asked, holding up the mug.

"No," she said absently, turning back to her screen.

Alex read over her shoulder. Her words were eloquent and informative. He could tell that she had put her heart and soul into this story, and he realized just how good she was at her job. He also noted that she had found a way to convey the story without giving vampires away and he silently applauded her for that. "That's really good."

She looked up at him. "Really? You think so?"

"Yeah, I do. I never realized just how talented you are."

Leaning over she kissed him. "Thank you."

"Ahem!" They both looked up at the interruption to find Sam leaning against the door jam. "Sorry to intrude, but I wanted to let you know that I just got off the phone with The Council. They have Roman in custody and they will be passing judgment on him shortly. I also explained to them the situation with Dimitri and how I witnessed you killing him out of self-defense. They agreed that no actions will be taken against you for taking the life of one of our own. It is officially over."

"Oh, thank god." Celeste clapped her hands together then gave Alex another kiss.

"Well…" Sam said, straightening. "Since my work is done here I better be heading out."

Both Alex and Celeste rose and walked Sam to the door. Once there they all stopped to say their goodbyes. Celeste gave Sam a big hug and thanked him for everything, insisting that he come back and visit soon.

Alex gave Sam a firm handshake. "Celeste is right. You should come back and visit. Maybe next time there won't be a crazed killer on the loose."

Sam laughed. "That sounds like a plan." Reaching for the doorknob he opened the door and walked out, giving a little wave over his shoulder as he headed down the front walkway.

Alex closed the door and turned back to Celeste. She stood looking at him expectantly, as if she knew he was about to say something.

He hesitated a moment, taking in the sight of her. Here was a beautiful, smart, and strong woman. Someone who just last night was kidnapped and almost killed, and now stood before him as though nothing had happened. As though it was just another day. He knew that he would never find another woman like her, and he didn't want to try.

Cupping her face in his hands he stared into her eyes and asked, "will you marry me?"

A look of shock briefly crossed her face then tears welled up in her eyes. Alex thought she would say no and for a moment sheer panic gripped him. Then, a wide grin crossed her face and she stammered, "ye…yes!" as she threw her arms around his neck and kissed him long and hard.

The heart that Alex was certain he didn't have swelled and overflowed at her words. Returning her kiss, he picked her up and spun her around.

When he placed her back on her feet she looked up at him and said, "you do know what you're getting yourself into, right?"

"Oh, I have an idea."

She smiled mischievously, "well, just wait until you meet my family. They are going to think we are crazy getting engage after we've only known each other for such a short time." She threw her head back and laughed, the sound like music to his ears.

Feeling the same giddiness she was, he unexpectedly picked her up and tossed her over his shoulder. Slowly he climbed the stairs.

"Hey!" she said breathlessly. "What are you doing?"

"I was thinking we should start practicing."

"Practicing?"

"Yeah. For the honeymoon." He gave her a light smack on the butt and smiled. He knew at that moment she was rolling her eyes.

ABOUT THE AUTHOR

Jennifer Richardson lives on the East Coast where she is continuing to think up new ideas for future novels.